Cover art by Brenda Walter
Editing by Heather Hayden
Narration by Jay Dyess

D1385079

THE COWBOY'S BARGAIN BRIDE PAPERBACK

First edition. July 1, 2020.

Written by Jessie Gussman.

***Trigger Warning**: sensitive content, on page but not graphic, for anyone who has ever lost a child. There is also a fade-to-black scene, necessary for the plot, between an unmarried couple.*

Chapter 1

Boone hadn't done much line dancing in his life. Especially in North Dakota. But the harvest crew he worked on had spent more than a little time in Texas. Sometimes rainy days could drag, especially when six or eight men were stuck in a camper together.

He had to say, though, he'd never line-danced to classical music.

Not in Texas. Not in North Dakota.

But his brother Clay's wedding marked the first.

He'd been on his way to ask about the notice he'd just seen on the gym door about the Sweet Water Ranch, and a woman, being up for auction, and he hadn't intended to get sidetracked. But his good friend Abner had been surrounded by pretty much all the kids in attendance, most of whom Boone knew, and as Boone walked across the gymnasium floor to find his mother, his niece, Gina, had stepped out of line and grabbed his hand.

What was a man to do?

Maybe another, different kind of man could ignore his niece's pleading eyes. But he couldn't. Not today. Not on this special day of all days when her mother and father were finally getting married. It was the happiest day of Gina's little life so far. Boone couldn't spoil it.

Abner's eyes glinted as Boone stepped into line, dragged by Gina. Boone ignored him.

It might be Clay's wedding, but neither Clay nor his new wife, Reina, was pretentious, and Boone was dressed semi casually in new jeans and cowboy boots. A simple, dark blue button-down completed the outfit he'd worn as best man. Reina hadn't made anyone in the bridal party wear anything fancy, and Clay hadn't cared. He'd just wanted to be married.

2

But he couldn't seem to step away, and he did something he normally never did.

He butted in.

"Come on, lady. It looks a little more complicated than what it is. Plus, the idea is to let loose and have a little fun."

Her lips buttoned down tight. With her upswept hair and fancy dress that dipped in the front and flowed around her legs like a whisper, he doubted she'd planned on coming today, letting loose, and having fun.

Man, for some strange reason, he hoped that bare finger meant exactly what it was supposed to, despite the boy beside her.

"If you dance with us, just once," the boy glanced over at Boone, like they were two against one, "I'll even eat the skunkages you wanted me to."

"They're Brussels sprouts," the woman said stiffly, shifting her nose up.

Boone snorted. The reception was potluck, not the first such reception he'd attended. Still, he'd never heard of anyone bringing Brussels sprouts to a wedding. But he'd really never heard of anyone calling them "skunkages."

"Good name," he told the boy. He looked back at the woman. "I'll eat mine too, if you dance with us."

Her lips twitched. Good. She had a sense of humor. He had to admit a certain amount of reserve attracted him—he wasn't going to think of Angela and her wedding several weeks ago—even if he no longer believed any woman was exactly what she seemed.

"Whether you do, or whether you don't, eat your Brussels sprouts is none of my concern." The lady raised her brow at him before focusing back on her son. He was speaking before she could.

"Just one dance. Please, Mom?" The boy took hold of the lady's hand and bounced a little, making her dress shimmer.

That scent, elusive and expensive, drifted by again. Boone wanted to grab it, hold it, and examine it. Funny how it twisted his brain and made him want to touch the fancy lady.

"It's not as hard as it looks. I'll help you."

The boy gave him a grateful grin. Normally, Boone wouldn't even consider doing what he did next, without even thinking about it.

He took the lady's hand and spun her so she stood at his side.

He was pretty sure that line dances had names, but he didn't have a clue what they were. He wasn't that into it. But, thankfully, he and Abner had learned together, and he recognized the sequence that Abner had started. One they'd done a million times and one of the easiest ones to learn.

He'd never done it backward, though.

But he stepped and spun, snagging her other hand and starting the heel-toe sequence with the opposite foot he normally would.

Probably when someone was teaching another person to line dance, they did it side by side. That's how he and the rest of the harvest crew he'd been on had learned. But he couldn't resist the urge to touch the fancy lady, so, with both of her cool, slender hands in his much larger, much rougher ones, he danced backward, calling the moves but doing the opposite.

"Heel, heel, toe, toe, heel, toe, heel, toe."

He was halfway through before she even lifted her foot. He wasn't sure if she was going to go along with him or not. Subconsciously he knew it would be embarrassing if she got angry and stormed away, dragging her son behind her. Or, maybe worse, slapping his face, like he probably deserved, then storming away.

But there had been something in him, or maybe a subtle sign from the lady—the slightly lifted mouth or the little tightening around her eyes that spoke of insecurity—that had told him she wanted to dance but didn't have the confidence to do it on her own.

Not that the lady wasn't confident. She oozed it. But a lot of times, with people in general, the outside hid a softer, more vulnerable inside.

He thought it was definitely true for the fancy lady.

They went through the sequence, with the grapevines and quarter turns, six or seven times before the lady caught on—much faster than he had when he started, he had to admit.

He could be wrong, but he guessed the fancy lady could dance the kind of dance that was actually meant to go with the kind of music they were moving to.

He wouldn't have a clue. But he could see why a man might be inspired to learn. Line dancing didn't get them nearly close enough. He wanted some kind of dance where he pulled her waist to his and their hips moved in time while their breath mingled...

He missed a step. The fancy lady arched a slender brow at him and tilted her chin just so.

He grinned, imagining she wouldn't be quite so cool if she'd known what he'd been thinking.

She didn't smile back, but her look softened some. Her movements were becoming less robotic and more fluid. Another few songs to practice, and she'd be a good dancer, no doubt. Better than anyone he'd ever been on the floor with.

He forced himself to let go of one hand, but he kept hold of her left as he spun around in time, beside her where he belonged.

Boone had never danced while holding a woman's hand. His little brother Mav was the flirt in the family. More than once he'd gone up to a complete stranger and offered his hand. Boone had never seen the point. On the harvest crew, they moved around so much, and worked such long hours, the chance of seeing the same woman twice, let alone more, was almost nonexistent. Why bother?

Plus, there was always Angela in the back of his head.

But as of three weeks ago, she was wearing another man's ring. So, why not dance with the fancy lady with the swirly dress and the scent that made him feel like he could float.

He'd dance first. Then, he'd talk to his mother in a bit about the woman who was being auctioned off, along with her ranch, in two weeks. He'd thought owning Sweet Water Ranch was only a pipe dream, and maybe it still was, since if there were people with money there, he'd probably not be able to touch it. But it was worth it to him to try.

Fancy lady or no, as long as the woman up for auction didn't have a beard, or a six-shooter strapped to her hip, Boone was bidding on her. Not for the woman. One of those was pretty much like another. But for the Sweet Water Ranch.

THERE WEREN'T TOO MANY men who would push past the cool façade Roxie Peterson used as a shield. The tall cowboy, with his crisp blue shirt and dark blue daring eyes, hadn't even seemed to notice it.

He'd grabbed her hands and taught her to line dance, like she wasn't giving him her haughtiest attitude.

She was glad he had. She'd been trained in formal ballroom dancing and taken ten years of ballet as a child. It wasn't hard to pick up the steps.

She didn't usually have such a magnetic partner.

Ha. She'd never had a partner like the cowboy who was now beside her, although he hadn't dropped her hand.

His fingers were rough and dry as they held hers. Nowhere close to the soft, slightly warm and damp grips she was used to. Bryan's hands.

She shivered. The cowboy beside her noticed immediately and glanced down, never missing a step.

She ignored him. In two weeks, she was being sold to the highest bidder, according to the stipulations in her rather eccentric uncle's will.

Honestly, she didn't really care. She'd done the married thing.

Big fail.

How could being auctioned off be any worse?

At least that way, she'd keep Sweet Water Ranch, which she'd grown to love, and she'd have a safe, if slightly wild, place to raise her son.

The will stipulated she had to auction herself off and get married. It did not stipulate that she had to open her bedroom door to whomever won the auction. Her lawyer had assured her of that much. If he hadn't, she would have given up the ranch, and pride be darned, she'd have gone begging to her brother to keep her until she got a job. Although what in the world she'd do was anyone's guess.

Teach dance lessons, maybe.

The cowboy beside her moved with a fluid grace that was unexpected. He smelled like the big North Dakota sky, full of sunshine and promise. And his grin caused her heart to float like a cloud in that sky.

But she wasn't falling for a handsome man with smooth moves and a cute grin. She hoped her heart was paying attention. It jumped every time the man's hand slid across hers.

She wasn't free to act on her feelings, even if she wanted to. She'd committed to selling herself and her ranch at the auction in two weeks. Come hell or high water, that's what she'd be doing.

She stumbled as nerves clutched her insides and the walls of the gymnasium seemed to close in on her. She could do it. She *would* do it.

"Hey? Are you okay?" The man's voice, deep and filled with concern, pushed into her consciousness.

It eased the tightness in her chest a little but not nearly enough. She gasped for breath. "I'll be fine. I need to step out for a moment."

She expected to slip away from him and duck out the side door behind them, into the darkened hallway and the restroom around the corner.

But she didn't have a chance to slip away, because he pulled her to the small door. Her heart pounded in her chest, and blood swished through her ears. She needed to get out, get some space. Get ahold of herself.

She'd been married before and survived. Bryan had turned out to be a stranger after their marriage. The auction wasn't something she hadn't already been through.

But she hadn't had Spencer.

The door clacked. She barely noticed when he pulled her out. The hallway, dark and cool, helped her heated body and racing heart immediately.

The cowboy still held her hand, but he didn't impose on her space. She took slow, deep breaths, knowing the ball of wire in her stomach would loosen soon. Most of the time, she was fine, knowing that a serial killer was unlikely to have the money necessary to buy her ranch. And her. It would be a hardworking man. Probably an older one who'd had a lifetime to accumulate the necessary cash. He probably wouldn't even be interested in a wife, and marrying her would be something he had to do to get Sweet Water.

She was fine with that. The house was big enough for them each to have a wing to themselves. And when she inherited the money—after she'd been married for a year—she could always send Spencer to boarding school, in Switzerland, if necessary. If the man proved to be someone she didn't want her son around.

They just had to make it a year. The ranch was hers as soon as the auction was over and she was married. The money would be theirs, one year from that date, if they were still married and still living in North Dakota.

Stipulations that her lawyer could fight. But not without a lot of money. Money she didn't have.

She took one last breath and lifted her chin. The cowboy's eyes, dark gray in the dim light of the hallway, grabbed hers. Concern covered his face.

It eased some as her face lifted. He must have seen her determination. His own face cracked into a grin. "Haven't danced with too many women, but that's the first time I've almost killed one."

His voice was smooth and sent a shiver tiptoeing up her spine. She fought it. She'd grown up rubbing elbows with wealthy business associates, not only at business functions but also at charity galas and on million-dollar yachts, gated estates, and private islands. One suave cowboy, from Podunk, nowhere, standing in a dark public school hallway, was not going to bother her. Not even a little.

The shiver bumped into the back of her skull and trucked back down.

She tossed her head. "I wasn't even close to being dead."

"No," he murmured. "I don't think you were."

The hallway wasn't nearly cool enough. Tempted to fan her now heated face, Roxie balled one hand and tried to pull the other out of his grasp.

He lifted his arm, tugging her closer, even as she pulled her hand away.

"It is something I can help you with?" he asked softly, like he knew she wasn't used to showing weakness.

"No. It's something I have to go through on my own." She didn't know why she even gave him that much information.

"Life's more fun when you have a partner." He seemed surprised at the words that came out of his mouth.

"I'm getting a partner. In two weeks." She almost smiled. That definitely made him blink, and she thought he almost jerked back. But her humor was short-lived. He stepped even closer.

"Maybe your future partner ought to be here." He put a hand on her waist, taking her fingers with his other, in what would be, if she had her hand on his shoulder, Closed Position from her ballroom dancing lessons. "Then you wouldn't need me."

She wasn't sure if he were referring to the fact that she'd needed him to help her dance, or that she'd needed him to take her from the reception and give her time to ease the panic in her chest, or that she needed him now, as he pulled her closer until there was nothing but a prayer between them. He started swaying.

Moving away would be the smart move. But she didn't want to, and her hand was suddenly on his shoulder and her body moving naturally with his, her hips following the hips of the stranger in front of her.

She didn't even know his name.

She didn't want to.

She was about to get married to a complete and total stranger; she didn't even know *which* stranger.

The heat from the hand on her hip was a sweet burn that traveled up, heating the tight ball of her stomach and whipping her heart into an even faster rhythm.

If only a man like this would bid for her.

But she wasn't delusional. Or romantic. The odds of her having an honorable, straight man, who also wasn't hard to look at and who acted like she was precious and held her like she was valuable, whose touch made her body heat and whose voice sent shivers bumping up her spine...the odds of that being the kind of man she'd end up married to? Ha. Zero.

She pushed the prayer away, and their bodies touched. His eyes widened, and his jaw hardened.

A smile touched her lips. Eve's smile, from millennia ago. Her hand moved from his shoulder to his neck, lightly brushing the tanned skin above the collar of his shirt.

His body shuddered.

His eyes, uncertainty pulling at the edges, searched her face, like he was trying to figure out what she was doing. Or maybe what she wanted.

She didn't know.

Her body tightened; the panic that been pushed back, but not defeated, scratched to be let out.

His fingers flexed on her waist. Then a soft touch. It might have been meant as comfort, but it stroked the fires of her soul.

Maybe she did know what she wanted.

She'd never done what she was about to do. Never even considered. She'd been responsible all her life. Always doing the right thing. Going to the right school. Getting the right degree. Marrying the right man.

And two weeks from now, she was going to follow her uncle's will to the letter, in order to inherit her family's ranch and, eventually, the money. She'd looked at the will. There were pages and pages of stipulations for every contingency. If someone didn't bid. If she changed her mind. If the bidder didn't have enough money. There were even time limits. Yeah. She was locked in.

But tonight?

She stretched up.

By now, the cowboy's eyes were wary, like he knew something was going on.

She didn't know many men who would refuse what she was about to ask, but she didn't know many men like the one touching her now.

He lowered his head. Their cheeks skimmed, the roughness of his stubble sending a delicious shockwave through her chest, easing the tightness coiled there.

Her lips brushed his ear. "I know someplace we can go."

His breath hitched harshly, loud in the dim, silent hall. His entire body tensed, the hand on her waist squeezing hard.

Another harsh breath before his head shook, precluding the word that came out of his mouth.

"No."

But his head was still lowered.

Anxiety gripped her heart like six-inch nails digging into the soft tissue of her body. Panic spun, clawing at the back of her throat. Instinctively she knew the man in front of her could make it go away.

His head moved back and forth, but his body hadn't pulled back. When his face turned toward hers, she moved, touching their lips together.

Chapter 2

"**W**ake up, you idiot. What's wrong with you? You just blew half a load of chopped corn out on the ground. Get a grip, man."

Luke Petal's voice crackled over Boone's CB radio.

Boone ground his teeth together and grabbed the mic. "Sorry. I'm watching now."

"You're supposed to be watching this whole time. It's like you're zoned out." Luke's truck and trailer pulled away from Boone's chopper spout. "That was just corn. You need to wake up, or someone's gonna get hurt."

"I know. I'm good."

There was no answer as Luke pulled away. Why should there be? They worked with heavy equipment all day long. No one could afford to be as distracted as Boone had been all afternoon.

It was Sunday, the day after Clay's wedding. The whole harvest crew, all six guys, had helped clean up the gymnasium after Clay and Reina left the reception. Then they'd piled into their pickups and driven half the night to get to northeastern Colorado, where they were now and where they were running behind schedule, hence working on Sunday afternoon after attending services in the morning.

Clay had left Boone in charge for the time he'd be gone. Not long, probably. Reina and he could go away all they wanted this winter, but when the crops were ready to harvest, everything needed done at once, and Clay knew it. He'd spend some time with his bride, but he'd be back. Soon.

Boone flipped a switch as Mack pulled his rig up beside him and started the chopper, forcing himself to focus.

15

He'd never felt this ripped up before. Not only about what he'd done yesterday, but today he was five hundred miles away, with the pressure of being crew boss on his shoulders and the idea of Sweet Water Ranch being up for auction, an auction he'd planned to attend and bid at, with the off chance he'd win and marry a stranger to get that ranch, pushing guilt through his chest with every single beat of his heart.

What had he done?

Something stupid. No other words for it. By far, the stupidest thing he'd ever done. And there was nothing he could do to rectify anything.

He didn't even know her name.

Profanity rolled through his head, and he hit the steering wheel with his fist, sending sharp, welcome pain up his arm.

The chopper jerked. The view out his side window was completely obliterated by Mack's blue truck.

Mack's voice snapped over the radio. "Watch it, man! You almost ran into me." A short break before, "Slow down! What's wrong with you?"

Boone picked his boot up off the gas. Yesterday evening at his brother's wedding reception, he'd broken every standard he'd ever had for himself and he'd treated a woman in a way that he'd sworn he never would and cheapened an act that was holy and sacred to him.

He knew what the rest of the world did, and he didn't care. His standards weren't theirs. It had never mattered to him what everyone else thought and did; he'd known what he wanted and, more importantly, what he wanted to be, and he'd lived that way all his life, never paying attention to what everyone else did. They had every right in the world to choose what they wanted to be.

So did he.

And he'd deliberately made the choice to be something different. Something harder. Something more.

Until sixty minutes yesterday evening had changed everything, and he'd become what he'd always despised.

But that was only a small part of the problem.

It had been an amazing sixty minutes. For him.

But the woman had left.

He'd assumed he'd see her again at the reception as it wound down, as they cleaned up, and he'd have an actual conversation with her, find out her name. He wanted to apologize, go back and start things over the right way, have a second chance to be a better man.

But she was gone.

It had taken an hour or so for him to realize he wasn't going to get to see her. That she was gone and he didn't know her name, didn't have her number, and didn't know how to contact her, even if she lived in the area or was one of Reina's friends.

He'd almost asked his mother. But he might be twenty-seven years old, and had been earning a man's wage since he was seventeen on his first harvest crew, but there was no way he could look his mother in the eye after what he'd done.

She wouldn't be angry. But she'd be disappointed in him, no doubt. She'd raised him to control his animal urges. Ha. He'd seen dogs with more self-control than he'd shown with the woman who had drawn his eyes and body from the first.

Unfortunately, as the night wore on, and he methodically cleaned alongside his crew members, then as he'd sat behind the wheel of the crew cab and driven through the night to Colorado with his buddies and best friends in the truck beside him, all he could hear were the words of the woman as she said she was getting a partner in two weeks.

He had slept with a woman he'd never met before, he didn't know her name, and apparently, to make everything that much worse, she was getting married in two weeks.

The right-side window filled up with a truck bed, and Boone jerked the wheel to the left, frustrated about everything he'd done and even more frustrated that he couldn't seem to concentrate on his job this morning.

That had never been a problem before, either.

He grabbed his CB mic. "You're full. Stopping," he said to Mack.

They happened to be at the entrance to the field, and as the truck pulled away, Boone saw Abner swinging a long leg off a four-wheeler and start striding over toward the chopper.

He stopped and waited. Something was up, since Abner was supposed to be running the other chopper.

The door clicked as Abner hopped up the ladder and opened it in one smooth motion, like a man who'd spent years moving in and out of machinery.

"Broke down?" Boone asked, wondering why he hadn't said anything on the two-way.

"It's getting taken care of," Abner said easily as he settled into the dummy seat beside and behind Boone. "Figured I'd make a few rounds with you while I'm waiting. Been acting weird since the wedding yesterday, thought you might be sick."

"I'm fine." Boone jerked the hand lever into gear, something he normally didn't do, and engaged the chopper before he started back out the row.

He didn't need Abner to babysit him.

Or question him.

Well, he'd wanted to talk to Abner anyway, although that hour yesterday had shifted his whole life. He wasn't sure what to do, but he wasn't going to cry on Abner's shoulder.

"What do you think of the ranch I bought just north of Sweet Water?" he asked before Abner could start an interrogation. Not that Abner would. He was as tight-lipped as any of the guys about his past. He'd better not start interrogating Boone about his. Of course, yesterday afternoon wasn't exactly ancient history. And it was affecting his job performance and compromising the safety of the crew.

Abner had every right to pry.

"Think if I were looking to settle down, I'd want one just like it. Mighta bought it myself, if you hadn't beaten me to it," Abner said, just a hint of the Pennsylvania Dutch of his childhood coloring the hillbilly twang he'd picked up since his Amish community had settled in the rolling hills of Ohio, just north of the Kentucky border. That was all of his past Boone knew. He'd pried to find out that much, since he'd never heard anyone who spoke quite like Abner.

His answer was what Boone had been expecting. Back when Boone had bought it, not quite a year ago, Abner had said something similar.

"How would you feel about buying it from me?"

Abner snorted. It wasn't a snort of surprise. "You saw the Sweet Water Ranch auction paper."

Boone's youngest brother, Mav, pulled his rig in beside Boone, and they started out the field in tandem.

"If you're interested, I'll back off." Boone was surprised at how hard those words came. He already had a ranch, and it would suit him just fine. Why did he want to give that up for the off chance to have Sweet Water?

But he knew. He'd admired the Sweet Water Ranch all his life. He couldn't pass up the opportunity to own it.

"Nope." Abner stretched his long legs out, propping them on the door handle and crossing his worn driving boots at the ankle. "You gotta marry some girl to get it. From what I could gather, she was at the wedding yesterday, but when I looked around for someone matching her description, couldn't find anyone. I assumed she wasn't there after all." His eyes leveled at Boone. "You disappeared for a while."

Boone sure hoped his deep tan hid the flush that burned up his neck. He didn't say anything, because there was nothing to say. He'd done wrong, and it wasn't that he was afraid or ashamed to confess it. He wasn't a coward, and he'd stand up and take whatever flack he needed to. But he couldn't, wouldn't, cast shade on the woman that'd been with him.

Abner didn't pry. Boone had known he wouldn't. If he had, Boone would be all over his past like wet on rain. And Abner didn't talk about his past. Boone wasn't ashamed to use that against him.

"Been hearing on the radio a good bit today that you've not had your head in the game. Kinda figured whatever was going on yesterday was eating you today." Abner's casual tone hadn't changed.

"I'm not sure marrying some stranger would be worse than scouring the countryside, looking for love. Or, at the very least, trying to find some girl that doesn't carry a knife in her hand waiting to stab you in the back first chance she gets." The bitterness in Boone's tone was undesirable but not unexpected.

Maybe he'd done what he did yesterday because of Angela and what she'd done. He'd never had an illusion that Angela saw him as anything more than Clay's brother. But he'd definitely had illusions that she could.

She hadn't broken his heart, he was sure of it, but she had made him harder and more cynical. Of course, if being hard and cynical caused him to toss his morals aside and act like an animal in a small, dark room with a complete stranger, then maybe he'd better work on rectifying his heart issues.

"You'd marry a stranger to get Sweet Water Ranch?" Abner asked, only a hint of incredulity in his voice.

Unbidden, a teasing smile floated through his mind. A stumble and another grin as she learned the simple line dance steps. A lifted chin and a look of stubborn determination.

Man, right now he wasn't interested in marrying anyone else. He wanted to find *her*.

"Yeah, I would."

"You want me to buy your ranch, so you have the cash to put down at the auction."

That was one of the nicest things about Abner. He was perceptive. Annoyingly so, at times. But he didn't usually need things spelled out to him. And he wasn't afraid to act.

"Yeah."

"You sure?"

No. He wasn't. He wanted to find the woman from yesterday. "I'm sure."

"How much?" Abner asked, his feet dropping off the door. He straightened, all business.

Boone named the price he'd bought it for. He'd not made many improvements over the winter, and he wasn't trying to profit off his friend's generosity.

"Fair deal. I already have tentative approval at the bank for a little more, contingent on profit and loss statements and some other paperwork."

"I have what you need, probably."

"And I have a little under half to put down, so getting the money shouldn't be an issue. I'll get to work on it." Abner grabbed the mic. "Stop here, Mav. I'm getting out."

They'd come around the field, and the ATV Abner had borrowed from somewhere sat just a hundred yards away.

Abner stood, opening the door. "I'll be talking to ya." His serious eyes, dark under his hat brim, met Boone's. "Hope you're not making a big mistake. It isn't a small thing to make a vow before Almighty God."

A jolt, like his veins had turned into pulsing shocker wire, ran up through Boone's torso. "God knows I'm good for it."

He'd never get the woman from yesterday out of his head. Not just the hour they'd spent in the reading room that had been turned into a large supply closet. But her easy laugh, her stubborn determination, the pain that shadowed her eyes, and the hurt she tried to hide.

She'd drawn him to her from the very moment he'd set eyes on her, pulled him as sure as the sun would rise tomorrow.

But if he made vows to another woman, he'd keep them just as sure.

He just wasn't convinced he wanted to walk away without even trying to find her or wait for her to walk back into his life.

Still, she'd hinted that she was getting married, too. Maybe it was for the best.

Abner exited the machine without a backward glance.

Boone had accomplished what he wanted—he'd arranged for someone to buy his ranch and provide the necessary down payment he'd be expected to front at the auction. If he lost the bid, though, he'd be homeless.

Chapter 3

"No. Don't park that there," Roxie yelled over the beating of the tractor motor. She waved her arms because Bill, the driver, almost certainly couldn't hear her. If he couldn't hear her across the dinner table with almost total silence surrounding them, there wasn't much hope of him hearing her while he was sitting on the open-cab tractor with the motor running.

"Over there," Roxie hollered. "Line it up with that one." She motioned her hands in parallel lines.

Bill seemed to understand because the tractor started going in the direction she wanted.

Great. Every day, someone called and asked if they could add their equipment/cattle/other unspecified junk to the auction. She'd not turned anyone down yet. Probably because the more stuff that had to be sold before she was sold—how odd to think of herself as being sold, even though she'd known it was going to happen since her brother, Ryder, got married—the longer it would be before she actually had to stand on the auction block.

Maybe everyone would go home before they got to her.

She wasn't sure what would happen then. She should sic her lawyer on that. He had the will with the twenty pages or more of contingencies. A legal solution for every loophole that could open. What happened if there was no buyer for her at the auction?

Could she bid on herself?

Possibly, but even the most modern thinkers wouldn't say she could marry herself.

Okay, maybe they would, but it wouldn't satisfy the specific conditions in the will, so as much as she would be willing to become a modern thinker, in name if not spirit, just to get out of having to marry a man not of her choosing, there was no benefit, so she wouldn't stoop to the degradation.

The cowboy from Reina and Clay's wedding flashed across her consciousness, as he'd done thousands of times a day for the last week. Nights were even worse. He took up residence in her mind and didn't leave until she crawled out of bed, fumbling for her robe and coffee.

He had a dimple in one cheek. A rather sexy cleft in his chin. As sure-footed and graceful as he'd been as he'd taught her to dance, he'd been slightly, adorably clumsy, although no less sure, later.

She shivered and lengthened her strides, heading toward the barn where she'd been cleaning the hay off the floor and fixing up an area where her sister-in-law, Nell, and her friend Elaine and their children had agreed to sell refreshments at the auction.

People might not care that the food was coming from a barn, but Roxie couldn't stand the thought of the place being dirty.

Plus, she needed something to do to take her mind off the cowboy from last Saturday. She was almost certain she could find out his name if she asked around enough. She almost had. After all, she was pretty sure he was with Preacher's harvest crew. But what was the point?

Yeah, he had a face she wouldn't mind looking into for the rest of her life, an easy grin, and skin, weathered by the sun and wind, that eased into familiar lines when he smiled.

He had the kind of integrity that said he'd keep his word if he gave it, and she was sure that what she'd talked him into on Saturday wasn't an activity he normally engaged in.

He had to have had girls make offers before. Which made her wonder why he'd changed his no to a yes for her.

She gave the broom an extra hard push and tried to do the same with Saturday's memories, even if they did make her feel warm and good in ways she'd never known were possible. Sure, the cowboy didn't have the smooth moves of most of the men she'd ever dealt with, and he definitely didn't have the arrogant knowledge of her ex-husband, but that was probably the pull.

Every move the cowboy had made had been more about her than himself. She'd never felt more cherished in her life. He'd treated her like she was precious and what they were doing was sacred, even though she'd only meant it to be a one-time, temporary fling.

He'd definitely given her the impression of a man who'd be looking her dad up—wouldn't he be disappointed—and wanting to "do the right thing" by her.

That wasn't what she'd intended at all, and she'd texted Nell about her son before running out of the reception and to the ranch to hide, which was very out of character for her, and lick her wounds, all self-inflicted.

The cowboy hadn't found her, if he'd even looked, and she should have been happy.

But, of course, she wasn't.

She'd done something stupid, and as happened every time, now she was paying for it.

She'd pretty much resigned herself to going through with the auction and holding up her end of the bargain. The first time she'd gotten married, she'd fancied herself in love, and look how that had worked out for her. So, why not marry for convenience?

But she couldn't get that cowboy out of her head, because he'd given her the first inkling that what her heart had always longed for might actually be possible this side of heaven. And maybe she could have it.

She only had a week before the auction, but she knew, as sure as she knew she'd die for her child, she knew if that cowboy came back, wanting to "do the right thing" by her...yeah. She'd let him.

THE FRIDAY NIGHT BEFORE the auction, Boone sat in Patty's Diner, feeling more conflicted than he'd ever felt in his life before. Up until this point, the decisions he'd had to make had been fairly straightforward. Black and white. Easy.

This decision didn't feel like the others. Abner had come through with the money to buy Boone's ranch. There were some final details and closing to happen, but he could bank on it.

So, the money wasn't an issue, unless the bids went way higher than he was thinking they would.

No. It wasn't the money. It was the woman. The one from Clay's wedding. The one he couldn't forget, couldn't get out of his head, couldn't walk away from.

But he would. He'd be at that auction tomorrow, and he'd be bidding on that ranch and the woman that went with it. And he'd put the woman from the wedding completely out of his head.

Except, he didn't think he could.

"Kinda nice that it decided to rain all weekend in Colorado." Abner took a drink of his water and leaned back in his chair.

Boy, Abner would never understand if Boone said he'd changed his mind about bidding at the auction. He'd either think Boone was unhinged, unable to make up his mind, or, knowing Abner, he'd guess exactly what was going on.

"Sure is. Clay couldn't have planned that better." Boone took a bite of his mashed potatoes.

"Next week looks clear the whole way through the weekend." Abner gave Boone a serious look. "Guess it won't matter to you, since you told Preacher you're done."

"I might not win the auction."

Abner pursed his lips and raised his brows.

Boone resisted the urge to squirm. Man, Abner had the dad look down. He didn't even try to play innocent. With that look, Abner could make him start confessing to things he didn't even do.

Bonne shrugged instead. "I told Clay I might not be back. And he was fine with it. He doesn't exactly have people beating the doors down to take my place." He tried for a bit of a subject change to take the focus off himself. "Are you going to the auction?"

"Planning on it. Might be some equipment in my price range."

"Cattle?"

"No. Not this winter. I might head to New Zealand again. I've got a spot on Luke's crew if I want it."

Boone nodded. Anyone would hire Abner. No one could outwork him.

"You know," Abner started then paused, his fork halfway to his mouth. "You can tell me to stuff it if you want, but the girl that you were dancing with at Preacher's wedding..." His voice trailed off.

Boone froze but was cognizant enough to try to act like he hadn't frozen, which probably made him look even more stiff and frozen.

"You just looked pretty natural with her." Abner lifted a shoulder. "I know you kind of fancied yourself as holding a torch for Angela. Don't judge every woman by the ones that are shallow and fake."

Boone's lip pulled back, but he didn't say anything. Abner hadn't said anything but the truth.

"It's not too late to change your mind about selling the ranch. I don't have my heart set on it, although I'd love to have it." He pushed a piece of meat around on his plate. "Some people never find that person that's the perfect fit for them. Some people let the chance slip away. Some people have it ripped away from them."

Boone figured he knew which category Abner belonged in.

"I'm not doing a very good job of saying it, and you weren't with that girl very long, but you were looking at her like a man should be looking at his wife. And she was looking at you like she didn't notice how ugly you were."

"Which is saying something," Boone said dryly.

"Sure is. If I hadn't seen that, I wouldn't be saying anything at all and figure you might as well roll the dice and marry a stranger. But you really want to give that up?"

Boone looked down at his plate. Advice from Abner wasn't something he'd take lightly.

Finally, he tilted his head back up. "You bidding on Sweet Water if I drop out?"

"Heck no." Abner's mouth closed in a straight line.

"If there wasn't a marriage clause?"

"I'd never have given you the money for your ranch."

"So, you've got a girl somewhere?" Boone felt he should at least be able to ask the question after the way Abner had just butted into his business.

There was a long pause while Abner looked over his shoulder. Finally he said softly, "No."

"Then why not bid?" Boone would step out if Abner wanted the ranch. Gladly. He'd wait until after harvest then find the woman from the wedding even if it took the whole winter. Except...she might be married.

This time, Abner was quiet so long, Boone was almost certain he wasn't going to answer.

"You ever love someone and hate them at the same time?" Abner finally said.

"Strong words." Love and hate.

"No," Abner said. "I don't have a girl. But it wouldn't be fair to bid on someone else."

Abner hadn't moved, but Boone felt his words like a line drive to the forehead. Abner wanted Sweet Water, too, but he was too honorable to bid on it because he wasn't free to give his heart. Even if the marriage didn't require it, it should at least be available.

Boone wasn't under the impression that he'd committed the unforgivable sin, but he was sure that he wasn't ready to walk into a marriage with what he'd done at Preacher's wedding so fresh. Plus, he was bare-ly a believer in love at all, let alone love at first sight, but the way he felt about the woman whose name he didn't even know was the closest thing he'd ever come to it.

Abner had helped him put things into perspective. There'd be other ranches and other chances. He didn't need to push for this one. Not with the messed-up way he was right now.

He scraped the last of the potatoes off his plate. He hadn't com-pletely decided, but he was pretty sure he wasn't going to the auction tomorrow night.

He stood, throwing some money on the table. "Pay my bill. I'm tak-ing a walk."

Abner didn't even look surprised.

Chapter 4

"So, does that mean that this guy, um, whoever he is, is going to be my dad?" Spencer looked at Roxie uncertainly.

Her heart squeezed like a wrung-out sponge. How did she answer that question? How did she do this without setting a bad example for her son, anyway?

It wasn't too late to back out.

Should she? Should she give up the family's ranch, Spencer's heritage, and wash her hands of it all?

"You have a real dad." Bryan. Even if he never called or visited. She was absolutely glad that he never wanted to take Spencer himself. "You won't need to call him anything you don't want to. Someone doesn't earn the title 'Dad' just because they marry a woman who has a child."

There. She didn't feel particularly wise, but she had to try. Maybe someday, she'd have enough wisdom that she'd stop making stupid mistakes.

Like the one at Preacher's wedding.

Yeah, definitely to the point where she was chalking that up to a massive mistake.

"But he's going to live with us?"

"He has to. That's part of your Uncle Edward's will."

"Can't you just tell the will no?" Spencer had a bit of a mulish look on his face. He had faults, like any child, but stubbornness wasn't usually one of them.

"Not really." She put a hand on each of his shoulders and looked him in the eye. "Do you have a problem with this?"

He'd known about the auction, of course, because he'd seen them getting ready for it. This was the first time that she'd told him she'd be getting married tomorrow night.

There'd been about ten potential bidders who had come to look the ranch over. She'd given Bill the job of showing them around.

Not one of them had asked about her.

She was sure of it, because she'd asked Bill after each one of them left.

No. They'd all been here for the ranch.

Spencer toed the ground with his sneaker.

She gave a light shake on his shoulders. "If you have a problem, I will stop everything. Right now. But we won't have Sweet Water anymore."

Spencer's lip pulled back. He loved the ranch. He didn't want to leave. "I want you to marry someone nice. Who doesn't yell at us. Someone who would take me fishing or let me drive the tractor, like Mr. Clay did sometimes. Someone fun. Like that guy who taught you to dance." Spencer shoved his hands in his pockets.

Roxie felt like he'd slapped her. How could she have thought that just any man would do? She should have listened to herself—just because a man married someone with a child didn't mean they became an automatic "dad."

But which was more important—the ranch or having the perfect dad, like such a thing existed?

She wasn't naïve. Perfect people weren't real. She, if anyone, should know that well. She'd been one of the people who looked perfect on the outside—perfect house, perfect car, perfect spouse and family—but it had all been show.

"You're my most important concern. Every decision I make is with your best interest at heart."

From the look on his face, he didn't believe her. There wasn't anything she could do to force him to, although it was entirely true.

Well, except for that really bad choice she'd made at the wedding.

She needed to forgive herself for that and move on. Except sin had a way of finding one out.

Her stomach curled, and she took a deep breath to clear it. She needed to get away and think. Somewhere where the panic would leave and she'd stop feeling physically ill every time she thought about how stupid she'd been.

What had possessed her? She'd never, ever done anything like that in her life before. Ever. Even in her younger, wilder days, when she'd lived the rich girl life to the hilt, she'd never been that bold.

Honestly, she'd never even been tempted.

It made her wonder what kind of person she really was. The first time temptation reared its seductive head, she gave in. Not only did she give in, but she became a Jezebel and led an honorable man astray, too.

The urge to throw up almost overcame her.

She dropped her hands from Spencer's shoulders. She needed to get away from the equipment and the people that were scurrying around, bringing last-minute items in and tagging equipment. People who'd stopped by and were now using their phone flashlights to check out the machinery lining the drive.

She swallowed, forcing her stomach contents down. For now.

"Mrs. Sprouse said she had a snack for you on the counter," Roxie said, referring to the housekeeper-nanny she'd hired several months ago. "She'll make sure you take a shower and brush your teeth, then you can play video games in your room until I get back home."

"Where're you going?" Spencer asked, a line appearing between his brows. Roxie very seldom left the ranch and almost always took Spencer with her.

"Well, I have some big decisions to make, and I need some space to think." That was true. She wanted space where she wouldn't have to be face-to-face with what was supposed to happen tomorrow. She also needed to get a grip on the nausea-inducing anxiety that burned in her gut.

Roxie waited until Spencer walked up the back steps and into the house before pulling her phone out and texting Mrs. Sprouse, telling her of her plans.

She waited for a response before she slipped her phone in her pocket and got in her car. Where could she go that she wouldn't be bothered? That she would have time and space to think? She just wanted—needed—to be alone.

The perfect place came to mind, and she pointed the car toward town.

ROXIE BREATHED IN THE quiet peacefulness of the sanctuary. She'd remembered the church was never locked. It was perfect.

She'd thrown up in the bushes before she came in, which had helped to settle her stomach. Although it still felt tight, twisted. Probably a normal reaction for anyone who was expected to marry what would probably be a stranger tomorrow.

Her friend Michelle had told her that she'd heard Bryan bragging to a friend that he was thinking of coming out and buying her. She supposed that wouldn't be worse than a serial killer. Maybe equal.

Definitely it'd be better for someone to only want the ranch, although Bryan, so far, had been the only one who'd been interested in the auction solely for her.

She almost jumped out of her skin when the heavy back door creaked. A shaft of light brightened the vestibule, then it dimmed and the definite sound of the door closing reached her.

She took it back. She'd rather have Bryan than a serial killer.

If it were a friendly lady coming to decorate her Sunday school classroom or the pianist coming to practice, she'd hit the lights any second.

The sanctuary stayed dark. The only sound was Roxie's heart, desperately trying to escape her chest.

Then footsteps.

Not wanting to be interrupted, Roxie had left her cell phone in the car. It seemed like every time she set foot off the ranch, she became an idiot.

The opposite end of the bench she was sitting on creaked and moved slightly. Whoever it was weighed enough to move the pew. A man?

At this point, Roxie was fairly certain whoever it was wasn't there to hurt her and didn't realize she was in the church. She'd parked her car in the lot behind the church. He might have walked in from the sidewalk. She hadn't heard a motor.

Her nausea returned along with a sharp pain in her stomach.

She might as well tell them she was here. She took a deep breath. A familiar scent tracked into her lungs. Before she processed why it was familiar, she spoke. "I just want to let you know you're not alone here."

The person had jerked when she started speaking. They jerked again before she finished.

Two seconds ticked by. Then it hit her, like a subway train, why that scent was familiar. She gasped.

The cowboy from Clay's wedding. Or someone else who smelled like the North Dakota sky and wind and a strength that had nothing to do with physical muscles. Spicy and warm. Totally unique.

Her stomach churned, this time for a completely different reason.

"I tried to figure out where I might find you. This wasn't exactly my first guess." The cowboy's voice was just the way she remembered. Warm and rugged with just a little bit of humor.

Well, she'd needed to make a decision. She'd come to the church, not exactly saying a formal prayer, but God had heard the crying of her heart, apparently. Now she just needed a sign as to what she needed to do.

"I guess you're saying I don't belong here." If he were one of those men who held women to a higher standard than men, that was sign enough for her. She'd already been married to Bryan. She didn't need another mistake like that.

"No less than me." His voice was easy, but there was a note of guilt there that eased her mind a little.

There was a small pause. Then he spoke again. "You said you were getting married."

"Yes. Tomorrow."

He didn't move, but she could feel the shift in him.

Maybe she should have exposed the doubt and fear in her heart. Maybe she should have trusted him with her insecurity and the confusion she felt. Maybe she should have told him that she wanted to do the best thing for her son, but she just wasn't sure what that was anymore.

But what did she expect would happen if she did that? That he'd jump up and pledge his undying love and devotion? That he'd say he couldn't stop thinking about her and would do anything to have a chance with her?

Hardly.

She'd be happy with an offer to date and be like a normal couple and maybe have a chance to fall for a man who looked at her as more than the woman who came with the ranch and maybe, for once, feel like she might end up with someone she could trust to not walk over her heart but hold it safe, like a precious treasure.

She supposed that was just a dream for fairy tales. And she wasn't about to risk opening her heart. After all, she couldn't stop thinking about him, but he was obviously around here and hadn't looked her up.

Her heart begged her to believe differently. Maybe he'd come back to try to find her.

She could find out. She'd never been shy.

"Are you from around here?" Her voice sounded normal to her. Since she didn't normally do what she'd done with him, she wasn't sure exactly what the correct way to act afterwards was.

He didn't answer quickly. She liked that. He seemed like a man who weighed his words and only said the true ones.

"I owned a ranch just north of here. My buddy just bought it, and I'll be bidding on the Sweet Water Ranch tomorrow."

Her stomach, still feeling a little nauseous, dropped like the ball on New Year's—slow but unstopping. The rest of her body froze.

He sighed. "I probably don't have enough money to even touch it, but I can't not try."

He was another one of those guys—the ones who wanted the ranch and would marry a stranger for it.

Again her heart wanted to butt in, to say that this could be a good thing, that she'd wanted a man like this to bid.

But anger rose in her chest. He'd asked if she were still getting married, but he was planning to as well. And it hadn't been that long ago that he'd been with a stranger in a supply closet, even though he knew he might be getting married in a couple of weeks.

He didn't even realize he had marginalized her, with her, but that didn't stop the anger from making her throat hot, like a stove pipe.

Of course, she'd done the same thing. And she'd been the one to suggest it. To take his no and change his mind.

Her righteous anger deflated.

She was just looking for an excuse to be angry, she supposed, when the person she should be angry at was really herself.

"I don't usually do those kinds of things." His voice came out of the darkness more uncertain than it'd been.

"I could tell."

Oh, she shouldn't have said that. She knew it, too. Could feel him stiffen and pull away at her implied insult. But she allowed the words out, and even as they hung there, she wasn't sure she wanted to take them back.

She hadn't really meant to kick him. But she'd known he'd take it that way. And she wasn't going to explain. It was probably a result of her being hurt and wanting to lash out and hurt him, too.

His swallow echoed in the quiet church interior. "I've wanted to apologize. I...I am apologizing. I'm sorry. You deserved more respect than what I showed."

She flipped her hair over her shoulder, an unconscious gesture that bolstered her courage. "No need to apologize. You know as well as I do that I instigated it. You respected me by doing what I wanted."

"No."

His disagreement settled between them.

Honestly, she liked his idea better. It was right, based on laws given by their Creator. Her opinion was based on the norms of the culture around them. Shifty things at best.

Maybe she leaned on the Rock, while he seemed planted in it.

Her way was easier. Less guilt. Fewer restrictions. But it was a fake freedom that saw her ending up bound by guilt and shame. And she'd imposed that on him, too, because she'd led him into sin, just as surely as Eve had handed Adam the fruit.

It might have been eight thousand years ago, but Boone and Adam had a lot of things in common.

"I'm the one that owes you an apology." She wrung her hands together, grateful he couldn't see in the dark. "And...I'm sorry. I...used you. I...had a lot of pressure in my life, and I knew you could relieve that for an hour or so."

Again, she'd hurt him with her words, with her apology. Because it wasn't the whole truth. And the negative implications were loud and clear.

The air around him shifted again. She wouldn't have been surprised if he'd gotten up and walked out. Maybe that's what she wanted. Or maybe she just wanted to get him back because he'd turned out to be like everyone else who didn't care about the woman as long as they got the ranch.

Although, if he'd even been out to see the ranch, she'd missed it. Just as well. She might have found a gun and beaten him over the head with it.

He seemed to shift closer. "If I could take it back, I would. Just because I know it was something I shouldn't have done." He took a breath. "I almost wish... No. I wish I could have been better, less obviously inexperienced, less green, I guess. Because, even if you were using me, you were beautiful and amazing, and I wish I could have been for you what you were for me."

He shifted, standing. "I hope you have a nice wedding and a happy forever. Your husband is a fortunate man."

With a swirl of air, he was gone, leaving only his scent behind.

Her chest felt tight, and if she were a crying kind of person, she might have shed a few tears. She felt like it. But her stomach wobbled and swayed until she finally got up and went out and threw up in the bushes again.

Chapter 5

Saturday evening, Boone flew along the highway, no destination in mind. His chest didn't burn anymore from the woman's barely veiled insults in the church last night.

She'd basically said she hadn't been attracted to him; she'd just been using him, and he hadn't been any good anyway.

He'd been so consumed with guilt he'd never thought he'd been so bad she might have realized it was something he'd never done before.

Showed what he knew. He'd thought she'd been just as enraptured and mesmerized as him. Right. She'd just been using him. Probably planning to redecorate her dining room. Hopefully she hadn't been planning her wedding. Maybe she had. He was obviously no judge of women. First Angela, who'd been after his brother's money, now this woman, with whom he'd been as intimate as two humans could be and whose name he didn't even know.

A road sign flew by for an exit. He didn't even know which exit it was. Heck, he didn't even know if he were still in North Dakota.

Normally he'd be out on the ranch, beating fence posts in the ground or using a shovel to dig a hole for something, but since it was going to be Abner's, he didn't feel he had the right to take his frustration out doing something banal but brutally hard.

So he'd been driving. On an interstate somewhere. Embarrassed that he'd been played the fool by that woman. Frustrated that, despite what she'd said, he still had to stop himself from praying that she didn't go through with her wedding today. Angry that he'd managed to pick out another woman who wasn't what she seemed.

He'd said what he had about the ranch and the auction last night because after he heard that she was getting married today, he didn't want her thinking he was wandering around, pining for her. Even if that's exactly what he'd been doing. He'd been going to go into the church, pray about it, and then call his mom and find out the woman's name.

His phone rang. He almost didn't even move to look at it. He sure didn't feel like being civil to anyone right now.

But it might be his mom. His younger brothers were old enough to shoulder most of the responsibility of taking care of her and their small farm, but he still contributed money. Clay probably did too, as well as the rest of his brothers. Except Wilder. No one knew where Wilder was.

Only the thought that his mom might need him compelled him to reach across the seat and grab it from where he threw it.

His sister, Lark.

Okay, he'd do anything for his sisters, but especially Lark, who was only eighteen.

There was no hands-free in the old farm truck he drove—he usually drove one of Clay's harvest company trucks around and didn't have a nice truck of his own. He'd saved all his money and used it to buy the ranch that he'd sold to Abner.

He finally got the phone swiped. "Yeah."

"Why, Boone. You sound so happy and cheerful. I hardly recognized you."

She definitely lived up to her name. He'd never met a more bubbly, happy person. His lip tugged up. It was almost impossible to be down in Lark's presence.

"Did you want something?" Now he was being surly just because he was her older brother and it was in his job description to give her a hard time. "Or am I just the unlucky dude you decided to badger and annoy today?"

"Where are you? I thought you were going to the auction, and I wanted to hang out with you, you know, in case I wanted to buy some farm machinery or something and you can give me your expert opinion."

"That dairy dude you're working for needs his hired help to buy him farm equipment now? Not surprising with the price of milk in the toilet."

"Shut up and get over here and help me. Where're you at anyway? Probably down at the food stand. Rip yourself away from the pies and come tell me which tractor to buy."

"You're not seriously buying a tractor?"

"I called you because I thought you were the least likely to argue with me."

"I'm your brother. I think I get deported if I don't argue."

"Why don't you try it and see?"

"Nah. It's too cold in Canada."

Her hearty laugh sounded over the phone. "Good one, bro. Where are you? You gonna answer me this time?"

"If you'd stop yapping long enough for me to squeeze a breath in...actually, I already told you. I don't know."

"Right. And I assumed you weren't serious."

"Serious as a brain tumor."

"Stop being morbid. Some of us want to stay in a good mood."

"And some of us want to stay in our bad mood. I don't know where you get all moral and assume good moods are better than bad moods."

"Boone."

"All right, I'll help you out."

"Great! Bring me a piece of pie. I make better decisions when I'm eating sugar."

"I'm not there."

"I know you're not here. I'm here, and I can see that you're not."

"I'm here, and I can tell that I'm not there, but I'm not sure where here is, except I know it's a long ways from there, so I'm not going to be there, with or without pie, which is here to you."

"Boone." She sighed, a long-suffering sigh. Man, he loved his sisters. "Would you just help me figure out which tractor to buy?"

"Sure will."

"Thank you." She sounded relieved.

"None of them."

"Aargh!"

"Is that all you wanted?" Funny, but the conversation with Lark had lifted his bad mood.

"I'm buying a tractor. With or without your help."

"Seriously, sis..." He'd managed to get the map app up on his phone. "I'm in the middle of South Dakota right now, heading south. I can turn around at the next exit, but I doubt I'll be there in time to be much help with the tractor, but if you save me a couple pieces of pie, I'll do my best to help you out there."

"I can't believe I grew up with hair."

He snorted.

"I'd ask what you're doing in South Dakota, but I'm afraid your explanation would either degenerate into a here-and-there type discussion, or you'd be sidetracked by walking hamburgers."

"I actually am passing a field full of black Angus. I should stop for a burger. Great idea. Thanks."

"Yeah, like I said, total inability to concentrate. Never mind. I wanted the tractor to be a surprise for Jeb, but I'll just get him to help me."

"Wait." Boone slowed down for the exit, all joking gone. "You're buying a tractor...for...Jeb?"

"That's right," Lark said cheerfully, completely ignoring the warning in his tone.

"That man is older than me. At least thirty."

"He's turning thirty next week. Hence the tractor."

"Hence the tractor? You don't buy men tractors for their birthdays. Not unless..."

"Oh. I think I see a piece of pie. Or maybe that's cheesecake. Maybe it's pie, cheesecake, and a hamburger. That's there. I'm here. You're somewhere or nowhere, and no one knows where that is. So, when you find yourself, tell yourself I said goodbye."

She hung up.

Oh, boy. He'd been angry that the dairyman had seemed to bewitch his little sister to the point where she was, apparently, spending her savings on him. But upon further reflection, he thought with a bemused smile, maybe he should pity the dairyman instead.

There were no vehicles behind him, so when he reached the stop sign at the end of the ramp, he programmed the GPS of his phone for Sweet Water. Six hours away.

The auction would probably be over when he got there.

Still, somehow he could see with clarity now. Why couldn't he see this last night?

Probably because he'd been too wounded by her insults, which he deserved. But they'd blinded them to the bigger conclusion. Which was, of course, that he'd done what Abner had suggested. He'd talked to her. He'd found out she had only been using him and, most importantly, that she was getting married, probably already had gotten married.

There was no reason why he couldn't commit fully to Sweet Water and to the woman, whoever she was, that the winning bidder had to marry.

He could do it.

If he got there in time.

ROXIE WIPED THE SWEAT from her forehead and brushed her hands off on her jeans. She'd gotten the tables set up where people could sit and eat their refreshments and benches up where the majority of the auction would take place. Bill was parking cars that were arriving early, since the auction wasn't slated to start until six and it was only three.

She thought she'd have time for a nap and a shower. She wasn't much of a drinker, but she kind of wished she had something other than cold medicine that might give her a little relief from the unending anxiety that soured her stomach. She'd only thrown up once, though, which she thought was a win. Her breakfast had basically bounced out of her stomach and into the kitchen garbage can. She'd skipped lunch, so there had been no food to bounce. She'd been too busy to think about food anyway.

She pulled the back door open and stepped wearily through the office and into the cool, blessedly empty kitchen. Her face was hot and flushed, and her body weary.

She was thirsty but too tired to get a drink. Instead, she lay her cheek on the cool countertop and stared at the calendar on the far wall. A pretty scene that befitted a farm kitchen was up for September on the calendar. A duck leading her ducklings through green grass with a shining pond in the background. Peaceful and sweet.

Roxie closed her eyes.

They popped back open. Wide. Her body had stiffened, but her brain scrambled furiously. Today was the twenty-eighth of September.

She did some quick calculations before pulling her cheek off the counter. It was a little sweaty and stuck, coming up with a smooth tearing sound. She barely noticed, not taking her eyes off the calendar as she walked toward it, her hand out.

Clay's wedding had been two weeks ago on September 14th.

She tore the top page down, hiding the duck and her brood and exposing the month of August. Her mind whirled, but the fact was there.

She was late.

She swore. One whispered word that hung in the silence of the kitchen like vapor from the Grim Reaper.

Her chest pumped in and out. The blood drained out of her head, and her neck turned to ice.

Of course. Of course.

She knew what happened when a woman did what she'd done. She knew it. But for so long, it hadn't been something she needed to spend a moment thinking about. Not since long before her divorce. She'd been so consumed with the auction and the ranch and the money and her anxiety over everything that the will demanded of her and doing her best for Spencer that she hadn't given this a thought. Not one.

And she knew exactly what the cowboy's method of birth control was.

Abstinence was one hundred percent effective. Unless one had a daughter of Eve whispering in one's ear, begging for just this once. At that point, the point where the cowboy's no turned into a yes, the abstinence method became one hundred percent ineffective.

Now she had a problem to deal with.

She put a hand over her stomach. No. Not a problem. Never a problem. Her child would never consider herself a problem. Because it was a girl. Roxie was sure of it.

Her stomach wasn't any more settled than it had been all day, but her heart could almost explode from the fierceness of the love that swelled within her.

Maybe the stress had made her late. She glanced at the calendar again. One week. She was one week late, when she was never, ever late.

She had time to run to the C store. Oh, boy, wouldn't that look good? No one could convince her that wouldn't make the rounds. It would definitely affect her marketability. She was supposed to be auctioned and married today, and she'd be in town, buying a pregnancy test. She didn't have time to go to Rockerton.

Or did she?

No one said she had to be here for the beginning of the auction. Only for the end. Spencer was spending the weekend with Nell and

Vinton. Heck, she could take a nap, a leisurely shower, go to Rockerton, eat a nice meal—that she'd probably only throw up on the way home—and still be back in time for her part.

She'd worked her butt off because she needed the distraction. But she didn't need to be here, and she wouldn't be.

She kept her hand over her stomach as she walked slowly away from the calendar and toward the back stairs. Did this change things?

She could stop the auction. That was possible, right up until the auctioneer said sold.

Her legs felt like they weighed as much as two full water buckets, but she dragged them up the stairs.

It didn't really change things because she needed the money now more than ever. And there wasn't any better place in the world to raise her children. Both of them.

What about the cowboy?

He said he was bidding. She supposed, in her head, she had assumed he wouldn't have enough money to win. She'd seen some of the men who'd come to look at it. Big, fancy trucks with dark tinted windows and big hitches. Several of them had Texas license plates, and she assumed their money was from oil. One man had driven in a Mercedes with New York plates. He'd looked familiar as she studied him through the office window as Bill showed him around. Maybe she knew him. But that life seemed so far away from her now.

She'd decided last night, sitting in the church, to go through with it. She'd thought it was God's will. A baby wasn't going to change her mind. God had known about that last night, even if she hadn't had a clue.

The cowboy didn't seem to think about that either, which wasn't totally surprising. He'd obviously not lived a life where that thought had to be considered. He certainly hadn't asked her or hinted in any way.

He didn't know, and while part of her knew he'd want to, all of her couldn't handle that kind of complication and stress on top of all the other things she had going on.

The cowboy was not going to find out.

Chapter 6

Roxie stopped at the first convenience store off the Rockerton exit. By the time she'd showered, tried to nap—unsuccessfully because she was too keyed up to sleep—and had made the two-hour drive in, she'd worked herself into a frenzy.

Was she, or wasn't she?

Normally, with only half of a tank of gas, she'd fill up, even though it was enough to get her home. But she pushed her organized, cautious side away. Which, she reminded herself wryly, was how she got into this mess in the first place. She strode with long, sure strides into the store.

A quick glance around confirmed she didn't know any of the four people in the store.

She went to the spot with the contraceptives. Why did they put these things in the front, right out in the open?

Probably they were a hot item for teens.

She was a long way from that. In body, if not in spirit, as her position in front of the display confirmed.

She'd acted like an irresponsible teenager, so now she got to stand in the hot spot, feeling eight strange eyes boring into her neck and the back of her head.

She picked a long, rectangular box up. She needed one that would give her an answer *right now, right here*. Because she was going to pay for it and walk straight to the bathroom, and if everyone in the store knew exactly what she was doing, she didn't give a flip.

She'd never see any of them again anyway.

Feeling a presence behind her, she refused to allow herself to hurry. Whatever kid needed condoms could just wait. She was going to get the fastest, most accurate test in the store, and she didn't care if she had to sell her car in order to pay for it. She needed the fact. The accurate fact. And she needed it *now*.

The presence behind her moved to her side. She tried to ignore it, but her eyes skimmed from the box in her hand to the square-toed, low-heeled, well-worn cowboy boots beside her. Rugged jeans covered the uppers.

It didn't take her more than a second to recognize the scent when it hit her nose a short moment later. Like the victim in a horror movie, her eyes moved in slow motion up the long legs. Past the belt buckle and tight t-shirt. Up the square jaw with the day's worth of stubble on it and the muscle twitching in and out, keeping time with her pounding heart and labored breath.

Those blue eyes, shaded by the hat on his head, were staring at the box in her hand.

They moved from the box to her face, questions shifting in them. They went back to the box. This time when they landed on her face, the questions were gone. She wasn't sure what the emotion on his face was. Maybe, like colors on a palette all mixed together turn to an unrecognizable blob of no color, his emotions had done the same thing.

He held his hand out. Her brain hadn't kicked back into gear. That should have told her, if nothing else had, that she was definitely pregnant. A fetus used up at least half the brain cells in a woman's body for the entire pregnancy and years afterwards, and there was nothing she could do about it. She placed the box in his hand.

Their fingers touched, and it shocked her that the entire store didn't explode. It was a relief, though, too, because she didn't want to make headlines by giving birth in a jail cell.

He felt it too. She saw it in his face before he looked back down and let his eyes linger on the bare third finger of her left hand. His eyes narrowed slightly before he pulled the box away and walked toward the register.

The four people who had been in the store were all still there. Still in the exact same spots. None of them were even pretending to still be shopping for anything.

If Roxie had to guess, they'd probably all forgotten what they'd come in for.

The store clerk didn't even smirk as the tall cowboy stood in front of him, buying a pregnancy test. He didn't manage to ask if the cowboy wanted a bag or tell him to have a nice day. Even the music that usually blasted out of the speakers of C stores everywhere was silent as a grave on Christmas Eve.

The cowboy turned and walked the few short steps back to her, handing her the box he'd just purchased.

Their eyes met. Betrayal was now clear in his. Surely he understood that the fact that she was purchasing the box meant she didn't know, wasn't sure, hadn't known last night when they "talked."

But no, of course he didn't know. Not only could he not read her mind, but he wasn't the kind of man who would have any experience in what they were now going through. She'd really turned his life upside down.

Knowing there was no way she could keep knowledge of the baby from him, she took the box and walked to the restroom.

He followed her. She felt his presence and his eyes as well as heard the soft thunk of his boots. She didn't acknowledge him at all before she disappeared into the cold, impersonal walls of the C store restroom.

BOONE STOOD WITH HIS arms folded over his chest, his back against the wall, his boots crossed at the ankle. His heart pounded, and his hands were sweating. He didn't care how stalkerish it was, he couldn't move his eyes from the opening of the woman's restroom.

He still felt like he was having an out-of-body experience. Still hadn't quite wrapped his brain around the fact that...he'd had a one-night stand. That he was about to become a father out of wedlock. That he didn't even know the name of the mother of his baby.

It's like God had picked him up by the scruff of the neck and set him down in someone else's life.

One good thing...the woman he'd slept with was apparently still unmarried. Was he the reason?

Man, his entire family would run each other over trying to be the first one to kill him.

Hard on the heels of that thought was the idea of the disappointment or, maybe worse, hurt on his mother's face.

His dad had died when he was young, but he'd always kind of thought his dad would have been proud of him. If not proud, at least not ashamed.

He knew as sure as he stood on two feet that his dad wouldn't have wanted him to treat a woman the way he'd treated this one.

Was she ever coming out?

He stood there for what felt like forever, no closer to knowing what to do, what the woman would want to do—he didn't even know her—and really no closer to believing this was actually happening to him.

He supposed he'd thought he was going to get away with a little secret sin. Sure, he'd felt guilty, but he hadn't actually considered there might be real-world consequences. Not just for him—it was affecting the woman in the restroom a heck of a lot more—and from there, it spread to his mother and siblings, his niece, his friends.

Done beating himself up about it, he lifted his chin. He needed to figure out what to do and pay the price, whatever that was.

She appeared in the doorway. A loose blouse that brought out the amber of her eyes and slim jeans that hugged her legs the whole way to her ankles. She wore flats. Her feet stopped in the opening.

He dragged his eyes up, forcing them to meet hers.

She was pregnant. He could tell by the look on her face. She didn't need to hand him the little white stick she was holding, but she held it out, and he took it.

He'd read enough of the box to know that the two lines meant a positive result. His fingers tightened on the stick. He was going to be a father.

His mouth was dry, and he wasn't able to swallow. His voice would crack or squeak if he tried to talk, and he didn't know what to say, anyway.

He couldn't read her expression. Not happiness or excitement, which is what he'd have felt, no doubt, if they'd exchanged rings.

He remembered her laughing up at him. Her slightly snobby New York accent and her dress shimmering around her legs as he led her through the dance steps. He remembered later, too, with her breath on his ear and her fingers in his hair and the look on her face so beautiful and pure he felt like Superman.

She'd claimed it had been an act.

He didn't want to believe that.

He shifted the stick to his left hand and held out his right. "Name's Boone Stryker. We keep meeting in the oddest places."

Her lips curled up, and her eyes lost some of their pinched look. She tilted her head just a little, and some of the East Coast upper crust arrogance reentered her eyes. She lifted a brow at his hand then slipped her own cool fingers into his. He fought not to close his eyes as memories of their fingers threaded together entered his head.

"Roxane Peterson. Everyone calls me Roxie."

"Is that what you want?"

Her eyes fluttered like his question surprised her. "Roxie is fine."

"But you prefer Roxane."

She lifted a casual shoulder. "I do, but I'm not going to quibble over little details that don't matter."

Roxane suited her. "I'm glad I have a name to go with the face...and the memories."

Her eyes widened a little like she was surprised he'd go there.

He wasn't going to pretend it didn't happen, and he wasn't going to pretend that she had been anything but perfect in every way. Because it was the truth. He refused to make her feel badly, just because he'd been stupid.

"Yes," she said, ratcheting up the haughty in her tone. "I've always thought it was a good idea to know the name of my baby's father."

It was his turn to kick his lips up in a grin. If they could joke about this, they might be able to make it through. God was disappointed in their sin; Boone wasn't under any delusions about that. But Boone also highly suspected that beyond the disappointment, He was also laughing. He never doubted that God had a sense of humor. Boone's life in the last three weeks was living proof.

"I'd always hoped the mother of my baby would have just that kind of intelligent thoughts."

She smiled but ruined it by pulling both lips in and biting down on them. She shook her head, her façade cracking. "What are we going to do?" she whispered.

He hadn't thought their options were that awful. He'd run over a small rock the wrong way pulling into the C store, and he had a flat he needed to change. But obviously, he wasn't going to the auction anymore. He was homeless, but he did have money. He'd have a spread, maybe not exactly what he wanted but something, in less than a month.

His preference would be to get married, but he knew that wasn't really the way the rest of the world worked anymore.

Whatever she wanted. He'd do his best to make it happen.

"You didn't get married today." It was almost nine p.m. "Is this why?"

She shook her head. "I'm headed there now. I...I just realized a couple of hours ago, and I had to find out." He still held her hand, and she pulled it away. He let it go. More shocked than he could say. She was still getting married?

A shaky breath trembled past her lips. "I didn't know yesterday night in the church. I didn't even suspect. I was completely shocked today when I realized this might be true." She nodded at the stick he still held in his left hand.

"You can't love him." He said it flatly. But it was a question. If she loved the man she was marrying, if she truly wanted to get married, he'd walk away, disappear, if that's what she wanted. It wasn't what he wanted, but he wasn't going to ruin her entire life if he could help it.

"I..." She tried to swallow and couldn't seem to. "I..."

"If you loved him, you wouldn't have been with me." He didn't mean to growl, but that's how it came out.

Her mouth flattened, and if possible, her back straightened even more. She lifted one of those high society brows at him. "You're right. Two weeks ago, when I was with you, for the first time in a really long time, I did what I wanted instead of what I should have done. Now, tonight, I'm going to do what I should, instead of what I want."

He was trying to puzzle her words out when she brushed by him and strode toward the door. She wasn't just going to leave, was she? Just walk out of his life after announcing she was pregnant with his baby and heading out to marry another man? She wouldn't.

But, oh yes. She was.

It took about three seconds for his brain to get his feet to kick into gear. She was already in her car, backing out, when he hit the door at a jog, slamming it open and rushing through.

"Wait!" he yelled.

She didn't look at him. He thought it might be a tear on her cheek as he sprinted over, but Roxane didn't seem like the kind of woman who cried.

He made it to her door, unsure what he was going to do if she didn't stop or wind down her window.

Thankfully, she did both. But she didn't wait for him to speak.

"Listen," she said, her arrogancy gone but her east coast attitude still firmly in place. It made him want to smile and throttle her at the same time. "I have a son and now this baby. I need to do what's best for them. I've had a lot of hard decisions and pressure and stress, but I said I would do something, and last night in the church before you got there, I felt like God confirmed what I needed to do." She wouldn't meet his eyes but stared at a point past his shoulder. And that was a tear track on her cheek. "I'm driving to Sweet Water. The Sweet Water Ranch. If I do what my uncle's will stipulates, I'll be set to inherit the ranch and a billion dollars."

She must have seen the confusion on his face. "I'm the one that's up for auction tonight."

With that, she shoved her car into drive and pulled away.

His clenched fists weren't nearly enough to vent his frustration. He wanted to pound his head against something.

He'd decided to bid on the ranch. Funny how the Lord was braiding their stories together, except Boone had pulled a Jonah and run away. Thankfully, there were no man-eating fish in North Dakota.

Boone grunted a half-laugh and looked around. At least none that had found him yet.

He burst into action. He wasn't going to stand around waiting on one. If he was going to get that tire changed and go bid on the woman who was carrying his child, he'd better get moving.

Chapter 7

The place was lit up, looking like broad daylight. There hadn't been a single parking place, and Roxie ended up turning around and parking her car at the end of the driveway.

She'd had two hours to think on the way home. After a lot of stress and anxiety, the way this was going to work out was pretty obvious to her. God had orchestrated it. After all, what were the odds of her meeting Boone—it was nice to finally have a name for her cowboy—at that C store? Or at the church last night? Of all the places in Sweet Water they both could have gone to have a private talk with the Lord, it was crazy that they'd both ended up there.

The dancing at the wedding had probably been orchestrated by the Good Lord, too. What had come after had almost messed up everything, but God could still work it for good.

So, obviously, Boone would be pulling in shortly. He would bid for her and—by some miracle—win and declare his undying love. They'd get married and live happily ever after.

She had never been a fairy-tale-coming-true kind of person, but the way things were working out, she could almost become a believer.

Ha. Yep. She had it figured out.

Walking up the drive, she was kind of surprised that Boone hadn't caught up to her by now. She smiled. Yeah, Boone was the kind of guy who would drive five miles an hour under the speed limit. Well, he'd better not be late.

There were people milling around everywhere as the auctioneer droned on in the background. She recognized the cowboy who had been leading the line dance at Preacher's wedding leaning against the barn, his hat pulled down low, one boot on the ground, one knee bent with the boot resting against the side of the barn. She couldn't exactly tell with the shadow of his hat brim, but she thought she felt his eyes tracking her as she moved up the walk, greeting a few women who were standing in a circle.

She garnered a few odd looks, a few that looked like pity, and a few more that seemed to wonder if she was really going to go through with this. Those looks made her thankful that she'd not been here all evening.

Gee Gee, Preacher's daughter, came running up to her, trailed by Spencer and Vinton.

"Hey, Mom!" Spencer called. "Can we have races down the driveway? Vinton and Gee Gee got permission if it's okay with you."

It wasn't that long ago that she might have told Spencer no, that someone might hit him. But now, she shrugged. "Sure. Watch for cars." North Dakota had relaxed her, and she thought maybe that made her a better parent.

The kids ran off, and she looked back down the drive. No one was arriving. She moseyed over to the back of the crowd and leaned against a big tractor tire, wondering where they were in the auction.

"Hey, Roxie," someone whispered.

Roxie turned. A blond head poked out from behind the tractor tire on the other side. Lark, Preacher's sister.

Her mouth dropped.

Boone had introduced himself as Boone Stryker.

Stryker was Preacher's last name.

"Do you have a brother named Boone?" Roxie asked before Lark could say anything, which was a pretty big accomplishment considering that Lark was pretty and vivacious and seldom quiet.

"Sure do. Why?" Lark said cheerfully, if quietly, as she slipped around the end of the tractor.

Roxie'd been too shocked about the positive pregnancy test for the name to register at the C store.

"Just wondered."

Boone Stryker. She put a hand over her stomach. Would she have done what she did if she'd known it was Preacher's brother?

No. No way.

She didn't know another family in North Dakota who were more conservative. There had never been a hint of anything resembling rebellion or gossip related to their family. They were highly respected and regarded everywhere.

The father had died when the kids were small, and all the boys had worked to support Mrs. Stryker. The family didn't have a lot of money, although Clay owned the harvesting business...that's why she'd thought Boone was part of the crew.

There was no way he could afford to bid on her.

"I need to buy a tractor." Lark had reached her side, a notebook and a pen in her hand. "My brothers are all being jerks. As soon as they find out I want to buy it for Jeb's birthday, they act like I'm a deranged imbecile and tell me, in one way or another, that their best advice is to not buy one." Lark stuck her pointed chin out. "They're moving down this row of tractors next, just as soon as they're done selling those wagons and feeders. And I'm buying one." She nodded her head and stamped her foot. Then her shoulders drooped. "But I don't know which one." She tilted her head at Roxie. "Will you help me?"

All spring and summer since Roxie had moved to Sweet Water, she'd heard Mrs. Stryker say, "The quickest way to forget your own problems is to help someone else." Well, this was definitely a Godsend to get her mind off her own problems.

She pulled her phone out of her pocket. "I don't know a thing about tractors, but I'm sure all the information we need is on the internet." She swiped, and her phone powered on. "Now, what does he use the tractor for?"

Roxie worked with Lark for a good thirty minutes while the auction continued behind them. They finally narrowed it down to an older

John Deere that Lark was pretty sure she could afford and a newer IH that she wasn't sure she had enough cash for.

"That's perfect!" Lark said. "Just in time, too. This is the last row." She bit her lip, and her smiling face straightened, immediately making her seem much older. Roxie guessed that a lot of people underestimated Lark because of her perpetual cheerfulness. "Are you ready?" Concern wrinkled her brow.

"I don't know how one gets ready for this. But I've been telling myself in ten years I'll look back and laugh."

Just like that, Lark's face brightened again, and she giggled. "Great attitude!" She shoved the notebook under her arm. "I have someone who's going to distract Jeb, but I need to go let him know which tractors he needs to have Jeb disappearing on."

"Isn't he here to buy a tractor?" If he needed one, that would make sense. Roxie scanned the crowd, looking for the man she'd seen only once or twice in town.

"No. The milk price has hit a record low every week this year, and he can barely afford to pay his bills."

"Then why's he here?" Roxie asked, finally finding him. A solidly set man with shoulders and torso that reminded her of a draft horse. He stood at the far edge of the crowd, slightly alone. Everyone around him was focused on the auction. Jeb stared at Lark. Although when Lark lifted her head, he shifted so fast Roxie almost thought she imagined it.

"Entertainment. In case you haven't noticed, there's not much going on in North Dakota. Why do you think your driveway and yard are packed full of cars? You think all these people are actually here to buy stuff?"

Yeah, she had thought that. "No. Of course not."

"Well, neither is Jeb. He's kinda shy. Reminds me of Matthew Cuthbert in *Anne of Green Gables*." Lark gave a wistful glance in Jeb's direction. "Once you get to know him, he's actually really funny and sweet."

"He's a lot older than you."

"Why does everyone always point that out?" Lark sounded perky and irritated at the same time. Probably the only time in Roxie's life where she'd heard that combination. "He's going to be thirty on his birthday next week. I'm eighteen."

But because of her life and responsibilities, Lark was probably far more mature than the average American eighteen-year-old. Still.

"He looks like a nice guy, and you're really sweet to buy him a tractor." Roxie didn't know what else to say.

"Thanks. I hope I win at least one of these."

"I'm rooting for the green one. It's prettier." Roxie might have just helped her figure out which tractor would be the best fit on Jeb's dairy farm, but she still didn't know squat about tractors.

"I'd better run. I want to talk to my decoy and make sure they're on it." She took one step then stopped and turned. "Why did you ask about Boone?"

Lark caught her flat-footed. She couldn't think up a truth she wanted to tell.

"I danced with him at Preacher's wedding, but I didn't realize he was your brother."

"Oh?" Lark gave a short laugh. "Maybe he'll bid tonight. I remember when Mom first started working here, Boone fell in love with it. He was only about thirteen, but he said he was going to own it someday if he had to kill, steal, or bribe the mailman."

"Huh?"

"Yeah. Maybe that's why I always remembered it. Because he didn't make any sense." Her laugh floated on the air, and a certain shy cattleman shot covert eyes her way. Lark didn't notice as she hurried away.

The crowd shifted as the auctioneer moved to the tractor on the end.

Roxie had been sure of everything just a few moments ago, and now she was as uncertain as she'd ever been. Maybe it was hormones.

Lark had said that Boone had always wanted Sweet Water.

But he wasn't even here. She'd been keeping an eye on the driveway. No one had come. The auction was almost over.

Could she allow herself to be auctioned now?

An arm slipped around her, and Roxie barely kept from jumping.

"How are you doing?" Nell, her sister-in-law, asked.

Her hand was on her stomach. She dropped it. If and when people found out about her condition, she wanted to tell them, not have them guess it because she couldn't keep her hand from wanting to protect the child inside of her.

"I'm as good as can be expected." Nervousness and cold feet were natural. She'd already decided she'd married for love once and it had bit her in the teeth. Today, she was stepping out, doing things a little differently, hoping for a different result. Very reasonable.

Nell looked both ways and lowered her voice. "I looked at the books when Mrs. Auker went to the job johnny." She raised her brows. "Eight men are registered to bid on the ranch."

Oh, no. If someone had to be registered in order to bid, Boone had better hurry and show up.

She glanced around. Abner still leaned against the barn, his eyes shielded, arms still folded. He could have been a statue. Roxie figured if Boone had managed to slip by her without her seeing him, he'd probably end up with his friend at some point.

Abner was alone.

Then her eye caught on something familiar off to his right, and she looked again. She couldn't contain her gasp.

"What is it?" Nell asked immediately, concern covering her face.

"Bryan's here." Her ex. He had a friend with him, and she recognized him immediately, too. Cheston Stoner. When her husband had cheated on her, Cheston had been the wingman. He'd divorced his wife about the same time Bryan divorced her.

"Is that him in the skinny jeans and new-looking...are those hiking boots?"

He wore a shirt that was artfully unbuttoned and hair that was casually mussed and gelled into place. Cheston looked very similar, except his shirt was pink instead of white.

"Yes."

"Figured. They look like East Coast people."

Roxie tried to take some deep breaths, in and out. "When you looked at the books, I don't suppose you remember if there was a 'Cheston' listed?"

"Actually, Cheston was the first name. I didn't recognize most of the rest of them. There wasn't anyone that I knew." She shrugged. "I thought at least a local or two would try, but I think they saw the big money from out east and the oil money from down south and they knew they couldn't compete." She bit her lip, like she wasn't sure if she should have even said anything. "I'm sorry."

"It's not your fault. My uncle wrote the will."

"But it's because of me that you said you'd do this." Nell twisted her hands and turned away.

That was true. Her brother, Ryder, had been going to inherit the ranch and money when he got married at a fairy tale ball. He'd wanted to choose Nell and thought he had. But he'd been mistaken. He wasn't able to change his choice without losing the ranch and money and knowing when he did, the next stipulation of the will kicked in and Roxie had to go on the auction block. Roxie had told him she'd do it, which left him free to choose Nell and lose the ranch and money.

"I told my brother this the night of the ball, I think. I've tried marriage for love, and it didn't work out. It's almost a relief to have the choice taken from me." If she didn't care about the man she had to marry, it wouldn't hurt when he cheated on her.

She tried to give Nell a gentle smile. It felt more like a grimace. If Nell only knew the things she was hiding. "Of course I'm nervous. I was nervous on my last wedding day, too. It's perfectly normal to be nervous."

Nell nodded, still biting her lip. "Do you want me to sneak another peek at the books?"

Did she ever. But she might be better off not knowing. She'd probably be better off making a snap decision. Once the winning bidder was announced, and it was confirmed he had the cash to back up his bid, she had thirty minutes where she could choose to forfeit the ranch and the billion dollars and not marry the winner.

Then, all of this would be in vain, and she'd be homeless with two children to raise.

They moved out of the way as the auctioneer sold each tractor in the line. Roxie was happy to see that Lark had the winning bid on the IH tractor. She hoped Jeb was successfully diverted and everything worked out for Lark.

The time seemed to fly by. Nell and Ryder gave her a hug and left with Spencer and Vinton. She didn't know how things were going to turn out, but she didn't want Spencer to be hurt in any way if she could help it.

Finally, the auctioneer's helper, a native North Dakotan named Flynn, found her at the edge of the crowd.

"Just two more tractors, then it's your turn," he said in a wizened old voice. It suited his thin gray hair and slightly tilted posture, the kind that bespoke a man who'd done manual labor all his life and lived with a perpetual backache. "Let's get over here and get you up on the platform so folks can have a good look at ya."

Like a cow at auction. She hadn't been here the entire night, but she'd been standing in the crowd for over an hour. She'd also been home every single time someone had come to look the ranch over. Not one of the men had tried to talk to her.

Now she was supposed to stand up so everyone could have a "good look" at her. Like her looks should even matter.

No. She wasn't even going to go there. She'd agreed to follow the stipulations of her uncle's will. She didn't have a whole lot of liking in her heart for her uncle, but he might have had reasons of his own. She'd finally been learning that when she sucked up her tendency to want to control everything and just let things work out, often they worked out better than she could have orchestrated herself.

She needed to relax and let it happen tonight. She had final veto power. It had to be enough.

Roxie was standing on the platform when the auctioneer hollered "sold" on the last tractor. Her hands were clasped in front of her, and her feet were set.

She hadn't eaten anything, so even though her stomach felt as rotten as hog slop crawling with maggots, she was pretty confident she wouldn't be throwing up. She hoped.

The crowd followed the auctioneer to the platform. It wasn't hard to notice that not a single person walked to their car and started out the driveway. Not one.

She supposed no one there, including her, had ever witnessed a person being sold at auction. It would probably never happen in their lifetime again. The local community center sold people for dates. She thought they'd even sold them for a day. But never for the lifetime commitment of marriage.

Of course, Bryan's idea of commitment had been slightly different than hers.

She put a calm look on her face and threw a net over the butterflies in her stomach. When the people here told the story to their grandkids, they were not going to say that she looked upset, scared, or weak.

She threw her shoulders back and lifted her chin. She'd survived the high society of New York City; she could survive this.

"And, ladies and gentlemen, we have the main attraction for this evening." The auctioneer spoke into the makeshift speaker system. Roxie heard his words twice. Once on the stage beside her, and once, after about a second delay, on the speakers that were scattered throughout the now trampled down yard.

"If all the men who have registered with the clerk and shown their bank references would please come forward."

Roxie's mouth was completely dry. She didn't even try to gather enough spit to swallow as seven—no, eight—men walked toward the front of the stage.

She kept her nose in the air and looked down at them. Cheston was among them. Smirking. There were three men with gray or thinning hair and varying degrees of potbellies. One of them had twinkling eyes. Another one looked kind in a grandfatherly way. The third limped a little and had a downturned mouth. Maybe he was just too nervous to smile.

She assumed they were the ranchers with money and any of those three would be just fine. They'd run the ranch, and she was fairly certain they'd give her free rein over the house and grounds. A marriage in name only, and she was fine with that.

Boone's image wanted to pop into her head, but she wouldn't let it. He knew where she was and what she was doing, and he'd said he wanted to bid at the auction. So he could be here if he wanted.

There were four slightly younger men. They would still be at least a decade, if not two, older than her. She figured those were the oil money guys.

Then Cheston. He was the only one her age.

And he was a multibillionaire. For him, it just depended on how bad he wanted her or the ranch or revenge or whatever it was. She wasn't under the illusion that he'd been carrying a torch for her all these years.

If he won, she was forfeiting. She didn't know what would happen at that point, to her or her children, but she wasn't going to marry Cheston. He was Bryan's evil twin.

The auctioneer started the bidding at three million dollars, and one of the old men bid right away.

Roxie looked out over the heads of the crowd, letting the auctioneer's singsong voice lull her into as much of a daze as a person could be in when they were standing on the auction block. So she noticed when the tractor trailer came over the hill and down the driveway toward the house and the auction. It was going a little faster than was safe, and there was absolutely no place for it to turn around.

It had to be lost, but all spring and summer that she lived here, they'd never had a truck get lost in their driveway.

Funny that the first should be tonight.

Crazy, loopy laughter wanted to bubble up from her dry throat, but she didn't want to scare the nice old men who were bidding against Cheston. They probably didn't want to be married to a lunatic, regardless of how big the house was.

The truck stopped, and the air hissed as the brakes came on. Because she couldn't look at the crowd, couldn't look at the bidders, couldn't look at the auctioneer, she was watching the truck.

Boone jumped down out of the cab, and at that point, Roxie wasn't even surprised. He'd broken down. That's why he hadn't been there. Of course.

He jogged over, straight to Abner. They spoke for a couple of minutes, then he turned...and punched the side of the barn.

Roxie couldn't help it; she did flinch at that. And her eyes got wide. Why wasn't he coming over to bid?

But then she heard the amount of money they were at—seven million—and she figured she knew.

He'd said he had a ranch, and he'd sold it. But there were no ranches nearby, and very few in the entire state, that were worth what Sweet Water was.

Boone couldn't afford it.

She kept her mouth closed and sucked a breath in through her nose, pulling her chin back up. Funny that her mouth was completely dry, but her eyes pricked and started to fill.

No.

She absolutely was not going to cry. Not now anyway. Maybe an hour from now she could cry the wrenching sobs that were backing up in her throat. More from the fact that Boone had wanted her than because he wasn't going to get her.

Or maybe it was all about the ranch for him, too.

She didn't care. If she had to pick out of all the people in front of her or even out of all the men in the world, Boone would be her top choice. At this point, it didn't matter if he only wanted the ranch.

"SOLD!" The auctioneer banged his gavel down on the makeshift stand. Roxie jumped. She didn't even know which man had won. She just knew it wasn't the right one.

Chapter 8

Boone should have known. He should have known he wouldn't be able to afford it. He'd been overconfident about his chances and underestimated the number and wealth of the people who were here.

Of course, until two hours ago, he hadn't really cared whether he won the auction or not. If he did, great. If he didn't, he'd be living with his mother for a while, but he had the money from the sale of his ranch along with his savings, and he'd find something to purchase before winter.

Now...now even the pain that throbbed up his arm from his ripped-up right hand wasn't enough to ease the pain in his heart.

Would she really marry that arrogant, cocky-looking dude that bought her?

He was powerless to stop her.

"No, you're not," Abner hissed in his ear.

Boone spun around to face him. "What are you talking about?" he hissed right back.

Abner pointed to the little white stick that was protruding out of Boone's front pocket. He'd forgotten about the pregnancy test.

"That guy might change his mind if he knows she's carrying your child."

Boone's jaw dropped, and his eyes skittered around. "How did you...?"

Abner's mouth tightened. "Go on. Swallow your pride and get up there. Before it's too late."

Boone gave Abner a hard look. Abner was right. Boone didn't want to get up in front of everyone and admit what he'd done. Lark was here. So was Clay. His mother. His other siblings and the guys he worked with. The town he lived in. People who had known and respected him all his life.

"Okay, folks."

Boone was already starting toward the stage when the auctioneer waved some papers around and spoke to the crowd. "Cheston, here, has checked out just fine with the finances. Now, according to the stipulations in the will, anyone in the crowd can object, just like at a real wedding, then Miss Roxie Peterson has thirty minutes to decide if she wants to go through with it."

Boone reached the stage and jumped up. "I object," he said in as loud of a voice as he could. His heart pounded, but his hands were steady. So was his gaze as it landed on Roxane.

Her eyes were wide, but they held resignation. Like she'd decided she was going to go through with it already.

Boone didn't have the money the other man did and couldn't provide for Roxie the way he could, and he wasn't sure exactly what his feelings for her were, let alone how she might feel about him. Maybe she hated him.

Regardless, he wasn't going to let her go without giving this his best shot. The crowd had become as still as moonlight at midnight when he hopped onto the platform. With the cool and uncharacteristic stillness of the North Dakota air, his voice would easily travel as the crowd waited with baited breath for what their native son had to say.

It wasn't what they were expecting; that was for sure.

He didn't step any closer to Roxie, even though he didn't want to stop until he was standing by her side.

Maybe she didn't want him there. Maybe she was happy to walk down the path she had chosen. But she'd told him where she was going and what was going to happen, and he had to believe it was because there might have been some small desire in her to have him here.

He didn't have enough money to buy her.

All he could do was use what he had, even if it shocked his friends, family, and neighbors. Even if it meant things that he'd rather keep secret were exposed.

He opened his mouth, hoping his heart didn't come out.

"I don't think she ought to marry someone else when she's pregnant with my child."

There was loaded silence for two seconds before the crowd gasped. Boone's entire being was focused on Roxie, but he heard it. There were a lot of strangers here tonight, but pretty much the entire population of Sweet Water and the surrounding area were here as well. He'd just let a lot of them down. But his concern was for Roxie. Her shoulders were back and her chin up. Pride stirred in his heart.

"Whatever," Cheston sneered behind him. "That's just an excuse she asked you to make." He lowered his voice. "Bryan said she was as cold as a dead fish. I can't believe she'd be overcome with sudden passion and take up with the likes of you."

The man, though shorter, looked down his nose at Boone. Which didn't bother Boone at all. It did, however, bother him that the man compared Roxie to a dead fish. He forced his fingers to relax out of the fist they had formed. He was already ripping his reputation to shreds; he didn't need to add an exclamation point in the form of a bare-knuckle brawl on the platform to it.

Roxie's eyes narrowed, and her lips flattened, a white line forming between them. Yeah, she wasn't too happy with him. He wasn't sure he was doing the right thing, and currently, she wasn't acting like a damsel who'd just had her white knight show up. Maybe she wanted to marry Cheston.

The auctioneer let his microphone fall to his side. He let his eyes slide between Boone and Cheston, finally settling on Cheston. "Is that going to change your mind?"

"He's lying."

Boone pulled the stick from his pocket. The receipt came with it. He handed it to Cheston.

Roxie opened her mouth. Before she could speak, a little man who'd been sitting on the platform, but in the back and off to the side, stood up and stepped forward. He held an official-looking folder.

Cheston didn't wait for him to speak. He shook his head. "Maybe there's oil under there, maybe there's not, but it's not worth this. I'm out." He strode off the stage.

The auctioneer put up a hand as though to stop him then shrugged. It wasn't his job to drag anyone to the altar, apparently.

The crowd parted, and Cheston disappeared. Boone didn't watch him go.

The auctioneer had probably thought he'd seen it all. To his credit, he only looked disconcerted for a moment before he glanced at the little man with the folder.

The auctioneer's singsong voice was gone as he said, "This is the lawyer who is here to make sure we follow the stipulations in the will." He jerked his chin at Roxie. "What do you say now, Mr. Peregrine?"

The lawyer adjusted his glasses. "It's not what do I say, it's what does the will say. That's the final word tonight. And..." He opened the folder he was holding. "It actually does have something to say about this situation."

The papers crackled as he shuffled them. "Ah, here. It says, 'If the buyer backs out, and there is someone else willing to claim the ranch and wed Roxane Peterson, then he must meet these specifications. He must wed Roxane Peterson within thirty minutes of the auction ending. He must live on the ranch with his wife. Neither he nor his wife will have access to any of the money of the ranch for sixty days, and at the end of sixty days, they must pass a test. The test will be administered by the lawyer who is executing the will. If they do not meet these conditions, they forfeit the money and the ranch.'"

The lawyer took off his glasses and looked between Roxie and Boone. "Are you two ready to keep those conditions?"

Boone waited for Roxie's nod. He didn't have to wait long.

His turn. "Yes." His voice was strong and sure. This is what he would have chosen the second everything clicked at the C store and he realized what her stand in front of the pregnancy tests indicated. He didn't care about the ranch, although he sure as heck wasn't going to pass on that opportunity, either.

"Then give me a minute to fill out the special license, and we'll proceed. I need your IDs."

Boone pulled his wallet out of his pocket while Roxie must have had her license ready, because she handed it directly over.

The crowd murmured in the background, but Boone didn't pay attention. His family would have some words for him, he was sure. Not because they hated him and wanted to make his life miserable but actually the opposite. They loved him. They wanted to help and encourage him to do right. Part of that was not allowing him to escape unscathed when he did things that would hurt him or someone else.

It's funny, though, the way God could take his mistake and work it for good. He'd have to remember to point that out to his mother.

He hoped it was good, anyway.

Roxie hadn't moved from her stance with her feet planted and her hands clasped in front of her. It couldn't be easy to be standing in front of all these people, knowing they were watching to see who would buy her. Maybe she was stiff because she'd crack if she weren't holding herself tightly together.

He wanted to protect her. To shield her from this. Instead, he'd made it worse.

His hands itched to reach out and hold her, but he wasn't going to get her trust tonight, even if he did make vows to her. It took more than a few words to earn trust back after it'd been broken like he'd just done.

He stepped closer to her, relieved she didn't back away, at least. Her expression wasn't hateful, but it wasn't welcoming, either.

"I'm sorry. I ruined your chance for Cheston. I didn't have time to check with you about what you wanted."

"None of this is about what I want." She didn't look at him.

"I, uh, I just did the only thing I could to try to stop everything and...get what I wanted." He wasn't used to being so vulnerable, and letting her know that he wanted her enough to stop the proceedings and announce embarrassing personal info that should have been kept between them was definitely making him uncomfortable.

But her lips flattened and she crossed her arms, almost like she was protecting herself from him. "Well, congratulations, it looks like two months of roughing it, and you might get a six-million-dollar ranch. Of course I come with it, but it's a big house, and you can have one side and I get the other."

His jaw jutted out, and his brows shot up. "That's not what I meant."

"Okay, you two. It's late, and these folks want to see a wedding before they go. You still both good?" The lawyer handed back their IDs and waved the special license in the air.

"I am," Boone said firmly. Although he was going to have a talk with Roxane just as soon as he could. He'd always wanted Sweet Water, never thought it would happen, either, but tonight wasn't about the ranch.

"Me too," she said, almost fatalistically, like she'd choose to get married to him rather than have her legs cut off at the knees.

They faced each other and joined right hands. She'd been married before, and maybe she'd had the white dress and flowers and fancy trimmings, but Boone still regretted that she was getting married to him on a cheap makeshift platform, surrounded by muddy fields and a whole gaggle of tractors and farm equipment. She wasn't even wearing a pretty dress. She certainly wasn't smiling.

He wished it were different. He'd change it if he could.

He made sure to say his vows loud and confidently. If there was another woman in the world who had a stronger effect on him than Roxane, he sure didn't want to meet her. He had all he could handle right here in front of him. He still didn't believe in love at first sight, although that would explain everything they did at Clay's wedding, but it wouldn't be hard for him to love her, if he didn't already.

The question was could the lady love him?

Her voice was softer as she repeated the promises that would bind them for a lifetime. Even if she left him, he wasn't the kind of man who'd switch boats midstream. He'd pledged his life to her, and he'd spend the rest of his life either walking beside her or walking alone.

"I now pronounce you man and wife. Sounds like you two already took care of the kissing part, so I'll present to you," he indicated the audience, "Mr. and Mrs. Boone Stryker."

"I'm not changing my name." Roxane's voice followed close on the heels of the lawyer's statement.

"Oh." The man looked crestfallen, like Roxane had given him a personal insult.

Boone was the one who'd been insulted. He kept his face impassive, though. He didn't want to fight about their names. It was probably a pride thing for him—he wanted his wife to have his name. Maybe it was a caveman thing where she was leaving her tribe and joining his, but yeah, that's what it said. They were joined.

But that's not what she wanted, and he tried hard not to take it personally, although most of the people he knew in the audience would feel the same way he did—like it was a slap in the face to him. If that's what it was, he was supposed to turn the other cheek.

He'd do that.

Tomorrow.

The crowd clapped and cheered, and some of them called for a kiss, but Roxane ignored them, and he did too. It was dawning on him that he'd actually done it. He'd gotten the woman he wanted, his child would be raised in his home, and Sweet Water was theirs as well.

But he didn't want to get everything he'd ever wanted and have Roxane pay. They needed to have a talk, and he would make sure that she understood they both needed to benefit from this arrangement, not just him.

"Okay, you two. I need you both to sign, then I'd say it's a wrap."

"That's great, because I have a headache and I'm going to bed." Roxane took the pen from the lawyer and used the folder to press on while she scribbled her name.

She handed the pen back to the lawyer without looking at Boone and walked toward the house.

Mr. Peregrine held the pen out. Boone took it and put his name, bold and confident on the line. He'd already said the vows. He'd put everything he had into making things work with Roxane. If everything he had wasn't enough, then he wouldn't live with regrets.

Chapter 9

Roxie hurried to the house. She'd wanted to pretend that Boone meant the words he was saying, that he wanted her and would have taken her without the ranch. She'd actually gotten excited, for the first time in a long time, when the lawyer said there were stipulations if the bidder backed out. Like maybe they would have lost the ranch and money, but Boone could have still chosen just her.

A picture flashed in her mind, Boone's head over hers, his eyes partly closed, and his lips skimming down, touching the line of her jaw so light and so soft that she barely felt it. A touch that spoke of reverence and wonder. The way one might touch a million-dollar vase. For a man who looked so rugged and capable, whose hands were calloused and whose skin was hardened by the sun and wind, it was the kind of touch that was unexpected.

It almost made her cry.

The memory made guilt prick her heart, sharp and sore, because she'd not treated him well out there in front of all those people. Being sold like a hog on the block, being looked at like a steer ready to butcher, being marginalized by a six-million-dollar ranch had made her feel worthless. A sideshow. Someone people came to gawk at and maybe even laugh at. Pity.

So she'd lashed out.

And he'd taken it.

Of course he had. He wasn't going to give up the ranch because of a few insults.

She was almost to the back door when someone grabbed her arm. She spun around. Bryan.

"You really knocked up?"

They'd been married, of course, but they hadn't seen each other for months, maybe a year or more. At least since she'd moved from New York this past spring. He'd cheated on her, so their divorce hadn't exactly been amicable, but really? No *hey, it's been a while, how are you?*

"Do you have anything you want to talk about that's actually your business?" She used her haughtiest tone. She didn't have to dig deep to find it. It was almost natural when she was talking to Bryan.

"I set you up with Cheston. He'd have been a good guy. What'd you throw it away for?"

"I think I heard Cheston mutter something about oil. I assume you paid someone to dig up old soil maps that might become relevant now that there is new technology to get it out of the ground." There was no point in pretending she didn't know what he'd been up to.

Now that she was turned around, she could see Boone standing in a group of five or six guys, several of whom had been bidding on the ranch. Beyond them, headlights were moving as people who had bought equipment and tractors loaded things up and moved them out.

Her eyes sought Boone out again and stayed there. He was tall and slim, with an easy stance and broad shoulders. He oozed confidence and capability, but there was also an innocence about him, a belief in righteousness, that couldn't be faked.

She thought of movies that depicted the Amish. There was just a way a woman who'd worn a dress all her life moved that actresses couldn't emulate. A look of innocence, the opposite of jadedness, that Hollywood couldn't fake.

Boone had that look. It made her stomach tighten and her blood feel like honey in her veins. That, combined with the way she already knew he would treat her, made guilt pinch even tighter.

She only needed to spend fifteen seconds with Bryan to know that, whatever Boone's motivation tonight, he'd never be like Bryan. She owed him an apology. Unfortunately she didn't seem to be able to make a solid decision and stick with it. Maybe it was hormones. Normally she was decisive and went after what she wanted. This whole auction and will had stripped that from her.

"You'll have to find that out for yourself," Bryan snapped, "because I'm not telling you. Where's my kid?"

"He's with friends. I didn't think he needed to see what went on tonight."

"I think you sent him away because you knew I was going to be here."

"How would I have known that?" She had full custody, but if Spencer wanted to visit his father, she had to allow it. If they couldn't work the logistics of that out, they had to go back to court. So far, it hadn't been an issue. Bryan hadn't spent much time with him, and Spencer didn't know him well enough to want to visit him.

He ignored her question, which didn't surprise her. "I'll be sending some lawyers around to make sure that everything that happened tonight was legit. If it wasn't..." Bryan gave a little shrug like how could he help it? "Then I suppose you two could stay married, but the money and the ranch should go to the highest bidder."

He didn't need to be making their lives miserable. That's all it was, since the attorney had just read from the will. But she kept her mouth closed. Bryan was all swagger and bluster. He didn't like to be shown up, and he wasn't afraid to throw money around, but his attention span was about three seconds long, and he'd forget about her before the next sparkly thing caught his eye. As long as she didn't provoke him.

Boone stood across the yard in the circle of men with his hands folded across his chest, his feet planted, listening with a thoughtful look on his face. He was in the light, and she was in shadow, so he probably couldn't see her staring. He looked good, and she was sure she wasn't the only female who was admiring him.

Luke—she thought he was from the harvest crew—and Boone's brother Mav came over, grabbing Boone by the shoulders and spinning him around. They were both talking at once, and Roxie guessed it probably had to do with what she'd talked him into doing.

Would he tell them he'd been seduced by a daughter of Eve? Somehow, she couldn't imagine it. She was almost certain Boone would keep his mouth closed and not say anything. But she couldn't watch, because she knew she was guilty.

She dragged her eyes away.

Bryan touched her arm. "I just want to make sure things are fair. And legal."

She pulled back, and his hand dropped. Words. That's all they were. He didn't give a fig about fair, and he didn't care about legal, either. Any more than it benefited him.

She tried to stop her negative thoughts. Maybe Bryan had changed. People did that all the time. She'd done it. She definitely wasn't the woman she was when she married him.

Giving him the benefit of the doubt was hard, especially after what he'd done, but she needed to try.

She didn't, however, need to stand here and listen to him. "I'm tired. Good night, Bryan."

Not giving him a chance to answer, she turned and walked up the steps and into the house.

BOONE'S MOTHER FOUND him before he'd been married for an hour.

He felt the firm hand on the small of his back while he talked with Clay and Reina. Clay had rescued him from Mav and Luke, who'd been bent on giving him a hard time, as he deserved. He hadn't argued back. What was there to say?

But his mother...

Clay and Reina melted away, leaving him alone with the woman who'd had seven children and one on the way when her husband died.

She'd changed his diapers, spanked his butt, driven him to the ER more times than he could count, and somewhere along the way, she had browbeaten a little bit of character and integrity into him.

To say she was strong and determined was to not give her nearly enough credit.

But he saw only love and forgiveness in her eyes.

"I'm sorry, Mom."

Her brows furrowed just a little as though she hadn't even wanted him to say that much.

"You know I'll love you no matter what. And you don't need to apologize. Not to me." The hand on his back slid around his waist, and he pulled her matronly figure close to his side.

She smelled like yeasty cinnamon, and her eyes glowed with love. It only made him feel worse.

He swallowed. "I know you will. And you know I do. You taught me better, and I didn't live up to the man you raised me to be."

She shook her head gently, her wrinkled, work-browned hand waving in the air. "Don't you know that no one is perfect? Don't you think I know it too? Surely you don't think I expect perfection from my children?"

"I expect myself to walk in this world, representing my God and my family and doing it in a way that none of you are ashamed to point at me and say, that's my kid."

"And you have." She pointed her finger and poked him in the chest. "That's my kid. You're going to be an amazing husband. And dad." She grinned. "I'm giving you a week, then I'm coming to butter up to my new daughter-in-law. I want her to drop that baby in my arms on her way out of the hospital."

Boone laughed. "You do not. But I'm sure you'll fight for snuggling rights."

"I will."

A promise to make sure she got them was on his lips, but he couldn't promise something he wasn't sure he could deliver.

"I hope I can make sure you get them."

Her brows drew down, and concern filled her eyes. "I guess I don't know all the details, but being that you've been gone all summer, that Roxie has been at Sweet Water every time I've worked in the office, and that I've never seen you two together, maybe you have a little romancing to do with your new wife?"

"Yeah." He wasn't going to go into the details. His mother had been very sweet and understanding, but he was pretty sure his actions at Clay's wedding would shock her. They still shocked him, to be honest.

"She's fierce, but she's loyal and honest." His mother nodded. "Your personalities are almost opposite, but I think you'll get along well." She shot him a sideways glance. "She's been in church all summer."

He looked over her head, unable to meet her eyes.

"I'm sure you'll see us." It was weird to think of himself as an "us."

"I'd better get going. Charlie wasn't interested in coming and stayed home to take care of the stock by herself. I can't believe she hasn't texted me asking where I was."

"You can tell her maybe she shouldn't have skipped the auction and she wouldn't have missed her brother's wedding."

His mother laughed. "Well, I hope it's your last wedding, but if you do do it again, maybe you could be slightly more traditional. Although the cheapness factor would make your Norwegian ancestors very proud."

"I'm all about cheap and making the ancestors proud."

He kissed his mother's cheek, and she patted his before she strode off. He was smiling, grateful that she'd taken the time to stop and talk to him. He felt a lot better knowing their relationship had not been ruined by his wrong actions.

It took until the wee hours of the morning to get everyone who wanted to take their purchases home organized and moved out. Boone hadn't been given any jobs, and the deed to the property wasn't in his name and wouldn't be for two months, but he still felt responsible. It was a good feeling, he had to admit.

There was still equipment and some animals in the barn whose purchasers were coming back to claim Sunday afternoon, but the last person had pulled out of the drive, and he and Roxane were alone in the house, aside from, he thought, the housekeeper.

The light gray sky promised a sunrise, the first of his marriage, as he walked into the house, hungry and tired. Their house. Roxane's and his.

Yesterday morning this time, he'd had no clue that today would start with his name linked to Roxane's and them sharing a house. He hadn't even known what her name was.

Bending down, he took his boots off, leaving them on the stoop. There was probably a place for them, but he'd figure that out later.

He had his stuff, what there was of it, in a few boxes at his old ranch. Of course, his pickup was still in Rockerton. He'd changed the tire, but it wouldn't start.

The truck driver who had brought him here, an owner-operator who lived just north of Sweet Water, had stopped to fuel then offered Boone his tools.

Boone had bummed a ride instead, figuring he didn't have time to fix whatever the problem was.

He walked through the office, familiar because his mother had worked here, part-time, for years, and on into the kitchen.

Roxane wasn't up yet, which didn't really surprise him.

He was hungry and thirsty, but he kept going.

He supposed he wanted to see Roxane. She'd be in bed, and he wasn't going to start opening bedroom doors just so he could find her and look at her, but he couldn't stop his feet from moving. Through the formal dining room, with its big, shiny wood table, and on into the living room, which looked out into the yard and beyond to the makeshift platform where he'd gotten married last night. It seemed like a dream.

Although, he supposed, in his dreams he'd never spent his wedding night the way he just had.

He was tired, but he didn't want to lie down, or he wouldn't be getting up for church. He didn't know if Roxane was planning on going, but he didn't want her going by herself on her first day as a married woman if she was. If she didn't, he'd go anyway. It'd sure be nice to have his wife beside him, but he had an idea Roxane wasn't going to be one of those kinds of wives that stood around trying to make their man look good.

Maybe she'd grow into it. He grinned. More likely he'd end up being Mr. Roxane. He'd reserve judgment on that idea.

He turned and moved from the window, thinking to check out the upstairs, where he'd never been, but he stopped when his eye caught on the couch.

Roxie lay there, sleeping, in the same clothes she'd worn last night, minus the shoes.

Maybe it was a good sign that she'd waited on him?

Or maybe she hadn't felt well.

He hoped that wasn't it. If it was, he should have been in here with her rather than out messing with the equipment. Man, married less than a day, and he'd already screwed up.

She lay on her side, her knees tucked up, her hands folded under her chin. There was a line between her brows like she had a headache or like she was thinking hard, even while sleeping. He hoped that line wasn't there because of him.

He didn't have any idea which room was hers, but he wanted to carry her up and put her to bed, easing that line between her eyes with a comfortable, familiar mattress and soft sheets.

Normally he wasn't wishy-washy in his decisions, but he wasn't sure she'd appreciate him touching her. She hadn't seemed overly thrilled about his interruption in the auction earlier, and it had to have been hard for her last night, knowing she had to get married but not knowing which man she'd end up with.

But she had that city-girl hardness, and she hadn't seemed scared. Not even a little. A man couldn't help but admire grit like that.

Still, it made him cautious, too. She might be lying on a shotgun.

Her eyes drifted open, just a second of hazy confusion before reality snapped them clear.

She started to push up, the line in her forehead deepening. Headache, for sure.

"I didn't mean to wake you. You can stay there. I just thought you might be more comfortable upstairs." He kept his voice low. Nothing worse than loud noises when a person had a headache.

"I need a drink." She kept pushing up.

"I'll get it."

"No, I have...other things I need to do."

He stepped back. Unsure, a feeling he wasn't used to and didn't like. He'd committed his life to this woman, and it was odd to think he was married to someone he didn't even know. Who he wasn't sure even liked him.

She headed toward the hall, slowly at first then moving more quickly, until she was almost running. He assumed she was headed toward a restroom. Of course.

The housekeeper wasn't up or about. Maybe she had Sundays off. Maybe she had off because of the auction. The amount of information he didn't know was frustrating.

Well, he was about to learn where the glasses were kept.

By the time she came out, white with a sheen of sweat, he had a glass of ice water and a cut lemon on the counter.

"Water?" he asked, nodding at it.

She shook her head. "Not ice. I need..." She swallowed heavily, swung around on her foot, and strode back out of the kitchen.

He'd been really sure last night when he'd been standing in front of the lawyer that marriage was something he could handle.

Now? It seemed it might be a little more complicated than he'd suspected.

Chapter 10

Roxie knelt in front of the toilet, one hand holding her hair, the other on the cool, porcelain back of the tank. At least she'd managed to get the water in the sink turned on this time. If Boone were standing outside the door, he wouldn't hear her gagging and retching, anyway. Not that there was much of anything coming up.

This was not exactly the way she'd pictured the morning after her wedding.

Probably not part of Boone's fantasies, either. And this was his first.

She couldn't help it, though. This was the worst she'd felt yet. And her head pounded and hurt to the point that she couldn't keep her forehead from wrinkling. She'd never felt a headache in her legs before, but the pain was so intense it seemed to echo down her thighs.

She'd seen her image in the mirror, and she looked like a college kid on a three-day drinking binge, while Boone, her...husband, looked like he could pose for the cover of a best-selling novel. She flushed the toilet and pushed off the floor, feeling weak and miserable and hardly able to keep her eyes open without her brain feeling like it was going to leak out. She definitely couldn't afford to lose any of it.

She washed her hands once more and wiped her face, carefully avoiding looking at herself. There was nothing she could do about her washed-out, pasty complexion. She hardly could bring herself to even care. She just wanted some pain pills and the ability to keep them down. And maybe a little relief from the nausea and throbbing, and at some point, she probably needed to figure out what in the world was going to happen with her marriage.

The idea of her...husband waiting in the kitchen made her stomach tighten again but thankfully not to the point of dropping her back on her knees.

She cleared her throat, straightened her spine, and reached for the door handle.

He was standing at almost the exact same spot, only this time she smelled coffee. The smell turned her stomach and made her throat spasm, but there wasn't anything in her stomach to come up, and she swallowed against the dry heaves.

"It's room temperature." The cowboy nodded his head at the water glass now on the counter. No ice.

It made her want to cry. She fought that urge with all the strength she had. Just what she needed on top of the spectacle she'd already made of herself. At this point, he had to be concerned he'd married a crazy woman.

She wasn't sure she could swallow water with the smell of coffee in her nose. But the pain medication was directly behind him in the cupboard over the stove. Normally she wasn't shy about saying what she wanted, but in the ten minutes she'd been up, she'd already thrown up twice and rejected his ice water. The man had to have a limit of what he could or would take.

Although he'd treated her with gentleness and consideration, the same way he'd treated her at the wedding.

Again, her eyes started to water.

"The pills are behind you, and I need them." Her voice squeaked some; she just couldn't help it. Her throat was tight, and she wasn't going to be able to hold the tears she didn't even know why she was crying for much longer.

His eyes widened, but he turned, digging through the cupboard and grabbing the bottle. "Two?"

"Yes," she said, adding a "please" on and hoping it didn't sound too much like begging.

He shook them out and held his hand out to her. His palm was big and rough, and she remembered how gentle it was and how carefully he'd treated her.

She fumbled, finally grabbing the pills, and swiped the glass of water off the counter. "I'm going back to bed," she managed to say as she turned, unable to stop the water from gushing out of her eyes, although she did stifle the sob that clogged her throat.

He had to stop being this nice to her. All it did was confirm that Clay's wedding hadn't been a fluke and that he'd truly shown her then the exact kind of man he was. Only she was miserable and mean and sick and ugly, and she didn't deserve him, and he'd figure that out soon, if he hadn't already, and he'd hate her and probably leave, then she could be miserable and lonely and pregnant alone.

By the time she got to the stairs, she was running, the water spilling out of the glass and her tears dripping off her chin. Her headache put a red haze over everything and bit into her skull with every step she took.

If he was gone when she woke up, it was nothing more than she deserved.

WHAT AN ARROGANT IDIOT he'd been.

Sure, for the last eight or so years, he'd spent six to eight months of the year bunking in a travel trailer with five or six other men. He could count the number of fights he'd been in on one finger, and before that, he'd grown up in a small house with seven siblings and his mother. He would have said his people skills were pretty darn good. He'd have said he was pretty easygoing, easy to get along with, and not easily provoked. He'd have said he could get along with pretty much anyone.

He'd have been wrong.

He'd never experienced hate quite like that before.

He walked into church, alone and late. It wasn't that he'd needed to be late, because he'd had plenty of time to go out, check the stock and feed it, and still shower and drive to town. But he'd not wanted to answer any questions. Not about his marriage. Not about his bride. Not about his wedding night. He'd wanted to avoid the smirks and knowing or questioning looks.

It would have been easier to stay home.

He wasn't big on "easier."

So he was in church. Heads swiveled when he came in, but he ignored them. He slid into the first available seat, not wanting to walk up the aisle and sit with his mother, Mav, and Charlie.

Clay sat with Gee Gee on one side of him and Reina tucked in close on the other. They did a little whispering and a little laughing, and he ran his hand up and down her arm.

Boone would be lying if he said he wasn't jealous. He hardly thought he'd have that with Roxane. Man, he couldn't even get the woman to talk to him. And he was pretty sure she was so upset she was crying when she finally ran out of the kitchen, and he'd be dipped if he even knew what he'd done.

Once, a few years ago, Mack had thrown a pretty big fit about someone buying, on accident, decaffeinated coffee. He'd tossed his cup in the sink and walked out of the travel trailer, but he'd walked back in five minutes later and apologized. It was the middle of harvest, and they all felt like they needed caffeine in the morning. No one was super happy, but they'd dealt with it and were laughing about it five minutes later.

She was pretty upset about the ice water.

He'd not seen Roxane again after she ran out of the kitchen. He'd kind of thought his marriage was going to be a little different than that. But whatever it ended up being, he'd have to be satisfied. Still, it'd be nice if she could figure out a way to at least be able to stand in his presence and talk about the weather or something.

The pastor kept speaking, and Boone hadn't even opened his Bible. He had no clue what book they were even in. Because the truth of the matter was his heart hurt. He didn't really think he was in love with Roxane. Surely not, but he liked her pretty good. It was hard to face how little she thought of him. Or maybe how miserable being forced to be married to him made her feel.

"Love is not selfish. If we claim to love someone, we show that by being willing to give up our desires for theirs." Pastor Houpe continued on, but Boone had caught just exactly the statement the Lord had wanted him to, apparently.

It's what he needed.

He wanted a marriage like Clay's. Like his parents had had. One where his wife looked at him with love and devotion in her eyes and he served her happily because she loved and admired him so fiercely. Where they laughed and worked together and their days were busy and full of chores and ranch life and their nights...their nights could be just like Clay's wedding, only he'd be less of an incompetent, awkward idiot and somehow better for her.

But...if that wasn't what she wanted, and it obviously wasn't, then wasn't he showing love, if that's what he felt, by giving up his dream—what he wanted—and doing what would make her happy?

He just wasn't sure what that was.

It wasn't him standing in her kitchen in the morning. Maybe she'd rather not see him at all.

Well, if that's what she wanted, she was going to have to stand him long enough to tell him about it.

He looked over, suddenly remembering the night they sat in the church and talked. Everything looked different in the daylight and especially on Sunday morning.

She hadn't seemed to hate him then. Of course, he hadn't interrupted her auction and forced her to marry him yet.

He sighed and looked back at the pulpit. He probably should ask someone for advice, but he supposed the Y chromosome kept that from being an option he would seriously consider. He'd rather figure it out on his own.

But, if he loved her, he'd give up what he wanted for her, right? So...if things didn't get better in a week, he'd ask his mom for advice when she came back to work.

Church let out not long after, and Boone chatted with his family and a few friends, most of whom asked if his wife was sick. He'd answered in the negative several times before he realized he really didn't know.

After leaving the church, he stopped at the diner and got a couple of sandwiches and a container of soup to go. He should have checked if they needed groceries, and he could have picked those up while he was out.

He couldn't use any of the ranch's money, but he had his own—what he'd earned for wages and what Abner had given him.

It was more than enough to get them through until whatever "test" they had.

His stomach tightened a little as he carried the food into the house, his Bible shoved under his arm. He managed to balance it in one hand while he opened the back door and walked through the office to the kitchen.

He stopped in the kitchen doorway and forgot to breathe.

Roxie sat at the bar, a mug of something—not coffee—in front of her. She looked up, her eyes uncertain. She'd been determined, confident, and bold. She didn't look any of those things right now. Boone wanted to find them and bring them back for her, but he didn't know how.

"Hi," he said, hoping and praying she didn't jump up and run out of the room. Again.

"Hey."

He stood there, feeling a little like a high schooler, although even then, he'd never had too much trouble talking to anyone. But he'd never liked anyone the way he liked Roxane. And wanted her to like him.

"It's nice out." Smooth. He couldn't even think of anything intelligent to say about the weather.

"Sunny." Either she was having the same problem, or she just wanted to be rid of him.

He stood there a little longer. Staring at her. Awkward.

Her eyes finally dropped. They seemed to run over his chest and shoulders before she studied her cup like it contained a message from...a boyfriend? Was that what Cheston was to her?

He wouldn't find out without asking.

Finally, he remembered the bag in his hand. He held it up. "I wasn't sure what you liked, but I brought a couple of burgers and some chicken noodle soup home from the diner."

Her eyes closed, and she took a breath like she could barely stand to look at him.

He was going to wait. Give her time. Let her talk to him. But he couldn't wait. His heart couldn't stand watching her force herself to be civil to him.

Striding to the bar, he set the bag of food on the edge and laid his Bible down along with it. He moved forward and put one hand on the bar beside her mug and one hand on the back of her barstool.

"What? Tell me what the issue is? Please?" He hated that he sounded like he was begging, but it tore him up to see her so upset she could hardly stand to look at him.

He'd made a decision. He believed it was the right one. Now, he forced the words out of his mouth. "If you don't want me here, just say so. I don't have to be in the house if you hate me that much. I can live in the barn." He grunted. "Trust me, I've slept in worse places."

Now her shoulders were shaking, and she had a hand on her forehead, one wrapped around her stomach. Man, she looked so miserable.

"Please...Roxie." He used the nickname that everyone else used, but it felt more tender and sweet on his tongue. Maybe it was another reason for her to be annoyed at him. "I'm sorry. I had no idea you wanted to marry Cheston that bad. You can't believe how badly I wish I'd never stepped in. I just thought...I just thought you'd rather have me."

He closed his eyes and dropped his head down. That wasn't entirely true, and he needed to tell her that.

"Okay. That's not true. It's not even close to being true. Last night, I wasn't giving a thought as to who you'd rather have. I just knew I wanted you for myself."

"You mean you wanted the ranch for yourself."

"No. I mean I wanted you."

"You don't want the ranch?'

"I do. Of course I do. But I'd walk away from it right now if you'll come with me."

"You'll walk away from Sweet Water?" For the first time, her face lifted from her mug. It was blotchy and red, and it looked like she'd been crying.

"If you come with me," he said, hardly realizing he spoke. Her eyes were a beautiful amber, clear but so full of hurt and pain that he couldn't stop his hand from moving from the chair and sliding down her hair to cup her cheek. Maybe she'd bat it away. Maybe she'd slap him, but he couldn't not touch her.

She seemed to believe that he'd bid because of the ranch. She'd said it several times now, and it finally dawned on him that it wasn't just something she was saying but that she actually believed it. He had to admit he'd dismissed the accusations because they were so crazy. To him.

Her eyes moved back to her cup, and he knew she wasn't going to answer.

He had to plead his case. "Would you look at me for a minute, please?" His voice was soft. There was anger in his chest. Anger that she could think that of him, but anger wasn't going to help him right now, and he shoved it aside. He wasn't typically the kind of man who got angry anyway.

Her head tilted up, and those eyes met his again. Memories of those eyes filled with emotions other than hurt ran through his head, and he had to shove that aside, too. He couldn't focus on his words if he started thinking about that.

"Do you think, even for a second, if that had been any other woman standing on the platform last night, up for bid, do you think, even for a second, that I would have bid on her? After what happened in the C store? Anyone but you?" His words were slow, and there was true, unadulterated wonder in his voice.

Her throat worked. She didn't look down, but her eyes dropped to his shoulder. Good. At least she was still listening.

"I thought you were getting married. Like a real wedding. I didn't know if you loved the guy or not, but I assumed that you were getting married because you wanted to. It didn't occur to me that you were the woman that went with the ranch. I guess I should have known it, and maybe I would have if I'd been working here all summer. But I wasn't, and I didn't."

He breathed out. He hadn't really said what he wanted to. Hadn't convinced her that he wouldn't have bid on anyone but her.

It would be easy to bring their baby into it. But even though he would have married her just to be a father and a family, that wasn't the real reason why he bid, either. Even if it had been the excuse he used.

His fingers slid off her cheek. Her eyes popped back to his. His hand that was on the bar moved over and touched her hand that lay by her mug.

He wasn't going to let things go where they'd gone before, but he wanted to touch her. She allowed his hand to cover hers.

"I wanted you. But I thought you were getting married. Where I come from, that would have put you off limits to me. So, maybe I still would have gone to the auction. Maybe I would have bid. But I would have only done it if I believed, because you'd told me, that there was no chance for me to be with you because you were married."

"Then let's walk away from Sweet Water." Her head lifted, and her serious gaze met his.

"You pick the place, and I'll work until I drop to provide for you and our children."

Her eyes flickered, and he was pretty sure he'd surprised her with the comment about their children. Spencer was part of their family too.

"Anywhere?"

"I love North Dakota, but it's more important to me that you're happy."

"New York?"

His heart dropped. Surely she was joking. Maybe she meant the state. There were farms in New York, surely.

He nodded slowly. "You want me to live in the city?" His hand tightened over hers. "Might end up in jail, 'cause I'm feeling constricted just talking about it, but if that's what you want."

"You'll leave Sweet Water and move to New York City."

"Can I hold my nose while I do it?"

"That wasn't a yes, cowboy."

His lip curved up. "Already said I'd do whatever you want, Boston."

"Boston?"

"You kinda look like a Boston. It has a nice ring to it, and—" He gave her a wink and a grin. "You're starting to act a little more like yourself, so when that full personality comes back from wherever it went, I can shorten it and call you Bossy."

She'd flinched a little when he referenced her missing sass and spunk, but it came back with a little gasp and a toss of her head.

"Well then, fine. I can tell you what to do. Slide the food over here and get me a spoon because I'm hungry."

He laughed, but he slid the food over and stood. "If we're not staying here, I'm not going to bother trying to figure out where everything is." He assumed the silverware was in a drawer. He opened four before he found it.

"I'm sorry, I don't know what's wrong with me. Maybe it was just all those other guys coming and looking at the ranch and not one of them tried to talk to me or acted like they cared at all. It was all about the money and owning Sweet Water."

His heart tugged toward her, hurting just a little.

He pulled out a spoon and shut the drawer. "Even Cheston?"

"No."

He set the spoon in front of her then took the lid off the soup and set that beside it, sliding it carefully into place while trying to form his question in just the right way. She seemed to be better than she had been, but he didn't want to do anything to set her off again until they got whatever it was worked out. "So...I got the impression last night and this morning that you were upset you ended up with me instead of Cheston." He spoke slowly, looking at her spoon until the very last word when he glanced at her to see her reaction.

She seemed shocked then appalled.

That made him feel better, but it also confused him.

"What made you think that?" she asked, her brows pulled tight together, the fire back in her eyes.

He smiled, just because that spirit was one of the things he admired in her. But he also raised a brow. "Maybe because you didn't seem happy that you got stuck with me. Last night, you didn't seem to like me at all, and this morning...this morning, I was pretty sure you hated me." He tilted his head. "I don't want you feeling stuck or feeling hate."

Her eyes narrowed. "I think you're serious."

"Dead straight."

"Cheston was a friend of my ex. He was, is, a philanderer too." Her eyes met his, straight on, like somehow she'd issued him a challenge.

"Guess that makes him my opposite," he said easily.

Her lips twitched, and she looked away.

That wasn't really a subject he enjoyed joking about, and he really didn't like her laughing about it, but it was what it was. He couldn't change it, might as well embrace it.

"Guess it's up to you now if I'm ever going to get better."

She looked at him from under her lashes. He couldn't read that look. It didn't matter. He wasn't getting the cart out of line again. He needed to get the horse to like him first.

"So, am I supposed to assume that you think you're better with me than Cheston?" he asked, just because he wanted to be clear. He'd been so sure she hated him.

She held her spoon suspended above her soup and stared at him. "I know I'm better with you. I just... I... It's stupid, but I'm sick of feeling like the ranch was the only thing that mattered."

"You still feel like that?"

"I think if we leave, it will solve that problem."

"Then let's go."

She gave a half laugh. "I'm not sure I want to leave."

"Well, if we stay, I'm not going to pretend that I'm not going to work on this ranch, as hard as I can, to make it the best that I can. But I'll do that wherever we go. I don't do things halfway."

A small smile tilted her lips. "I've figured that out."

"I kinda felt like you didn't, either."

"No. Usually I know exactly what I want, and I don't have a problem going after it."

So, yeah. Maybe his grin was a little wolfish. "Think I figured that out a few weeks ago."

Her smile faded, and she stirred her soup absently.

"Hey." He touched her hand. Eventually they'd have to talk about that. If she regretted it, she might be happy to hear that it wasn't his finest hour, either.

"I've never done anything like that before. I've always been a Type A and, yes, bossy. Organized. But I've never slept around."

"And you regret the action? Or you regret the consequence?" he asked, referring to their baby.

"The action, of course. I don't regret the baby other than the way she's complicated things." She pushed her half-eaten soup away. "One of the many complications is that I didn't hate you this morning. I was dealing with morning sickness, and I was embarrassed." She sighed. "And unsure, I guess, too."

He leaned against the back of the stool between them, thinking. "You're sick because you're pregnant."

"Yes. You know, morning sickness."

Chapter 11

Boone's face scrunched up.

It was adorable, and Roxie knew she was letting her guard down. She shouldn't. He insisted he wasn't after the ranch, and she knew she should believe him. All his actions had backed up the words he'd just uttered. But it was so hard to believe that someone could be as...nice as Boone seemed to be.

"I guess this is what we missed at the getting to know you stage." He reached in the bag and pulled out two containers, setting one in front of her and opening the other for himself. "I haven't been around women much. My two sisters are a good bit younger. Things people learn on TV or whatever, we never watched it. Didn't have time. No dad and a lot of mouths to feed." He grinned. "Some of us ate more than others." He nodded at her soup. "You done with that?"

She gave him an uncertain look. "Yes?" He was looking at it like he was planning on eating it.

Sure enough, he took it from in front of her and started to spoon it into his mouth. Okay, yeah, so they were married, but only for a few hours, and seriously, he was eating after an almost perfect stranger?

"Basically," he said, "if you're expecting me to know a bunch of stuff about women, I'm gonna disappoint you. Unless it's bovine related."

That really wasn't disappointing to her. Not much.

"So you need me to explain morning sickness?"

"Nooo." He drew his answer out. "I think I have it figured out. You're gonna be sick in the morning and act like you hate me because you're pregnant."

"I did not act like I hated you."

"So, obviously, you don't know much about men." He picked up his burger. "Let me clue you in. When you cry at the sight of me, it makes me think you hate me. I think that's a universal trait."

"I had a headache, and I was throwing up. I didn't cry at the sight of you." She picked up a fry.

He stood, walking to the refrigerator and returning with ketchup. He held it up with a questioning look.

"Please."

He squirted it on the lid of her container. "So you're not sick now?"

"No. I was last night. But that might have been nerves."

"You were nervous?" he asked incredulously.

"Yes. Absolutely. Wouldn't you have been?"

"I'd have walked. No way I'd agree to get married to a stranger unless I chose to."

"I told Ryder I would. It was the only way he'd let go and marry Nell."

As she figured he would, he nodded. He'd have done the same for any of his family; she was sure of it.

She allowed a little smile to touch her lips, still not ready to bare all of her feelings for him. "Plus, I'm not unhappy with the way it worked out. I've been learning, sometimes, when you let things go, rather than try to control everything, things work out better than you think they would."

There was humor in the crinkle of his eyes as he chewed on his hamburger and met her gaze. He swallowed. "A hard lesson, huh?"

She grunted. "I guess it's harder for some of us than others." He seemed like such a relaxed, easygoing person; he probably had no idea of her struggle.

"You know everyone has things they have to deal with or overcome in their personality."

"I know. I assume it would be so much easier, though, to have a personality like yours."

"Maybe if I were a little more forceful, more determined to get my way, I wouldn't have let you change my mind." He held his burger in front of his mouth. "I'm not really complaining, though. Think I won't mind a little bossiness."

He didn't say "in the bedroom," but she couldn't help but wonder if he thought it.

"I meant every word of the vows I said last night." His casual tone hadn't changed, but there was a new tension in his shoulders as he put the last of his burger in his mouth. He watched her, and she figured he wanted to know where she stood on their marriage, too.

She drew a fry through the ketchup, back and forth. The familiar stirring in her blood when Boone was around heated up. She wondered, exactly what he was thinking, how their marriage would play out.

She finally looked up. "I did too."

Maybe she imagined it, but she thought she saw relief in his eyes. "Then we have the rest of our lives. We started out kinda fast. Maybe we can back up and start again. Go a little slower this time?"

She thought she understood what he was saying, and the idea made her feel like their relationship was important to him. "What, exactly, do you mean by 'a little slower'?"

The cleft in his chin deepened when he smiled.

"Time frame," she added, because she wasn't sure he understood and she wasn't ready for any awkward physical descriptions.

"Couple months?" he said, scratching his chin. Then the humor slid from his face. "Do you have any idea what the lawyer meant when he said we'd have a test?"

"Well, I think he gave me a letter about it at some point. But basically, it's something that we have to pass to keep the ranch and money."

"Then we don't need to worry about it? You didn't seem like you cared about the ranch."

"I'm sure I did give that impression. It wasn't very nice of me to be pushing like that, but I wanted to test you, just to see if you'd fight to keep it."

"I suspected as much, but I was being dead serious. I like it, but I'm not attached to it. Not like I'm attached to you." He nodded at her half-eaten sandwich. "You finishing that?"

She pushed it toward him. "You're not even going to surprise me by eating it. Have my fries, too."

He laughed. "I should have gotten myself two." He pulled it toward him. "What does the test consist of? Multiple choice answers? Essay questions? Fitness activities? Roping steers?"

It was her turn to laugh. "I hope not. I'll not be very good at that."

"Eh, don't worry about it. I'll rope your steers, and you can answer my essay questions."

"Hmm. I really don't know. It's just going to be something that we have to pass. I think the letter said he'd be here to give it to us and we'd have a week to do it."

"I see. Well, if keeping the ranch and money is important to you, we'll figure out what to do to ace it, whatever it is."

In the time that she'd moved to Sweet Water, the ranch had felt like home. She'd noticed a huge difference in Spencer, and she wanted to raise the baby she was carrying here, too. It was a family thing. Something they'd had for generations. It made her proud to be part of it. "I'd like that."

"I think we've gotten the big stuff settled. I know what morning sickness is and that you don't hate me." She harrumphed. "We're both committed to staying married and trying to pass the test. You know I don't know anything about women." He stacked her empty container with his. "Oh, and I warned you that I was planning on a slow seduction campaign."

She waved her hand. "We're married. That's not necessary."

He stopped.

Her breath hitched as he turned toward her slowly. "Maybe I think it is. Maybe this isn't something I'm willing to compromise on. Maybe I think you're worth it and wish that I had done it right the first time."

Her heart slammed and jerked in her chest, and she had trouble looking him in the eye. He was too serious, too...too good to be true. She'd never met anyone else like him. Maybe because she hadn't lived in North Dakota, and there just weren't guys like this in the city. Or maybe it was just Boone. Whatever it was, it scared her. A little fling she could handle. Something that didn't scratch past the surface.

But Boone wanted more from her, and something told her he wasn't going to be satisfied until he had everything.

She wasn't sure she wanted to go down that road again.

She already knew his tenderness could make her cry. And she didn't want to be one of those weak women who melted at the sight of a man. She'd worked long and hard to become self-reliant and self-contained.

Just because she allowed herself to be sold at auction to fulfill her promise and the stipulations in her uncle's will didn't mean she was going to sell her heart and soul along with it.

He had stopped stacking their containers and watched her. His fingers came up and landed lightly on the edge of her jaw. "What?"

She forced a pleasant look, despite the war going on inside of her—her heart begging her to trust, her mind reminding her of Bryan's betrayal and the infidelity that occurred all around her on a regular basis when she was married and living in New York.

"Nothing." She shrugged and moved, and his hand fell down. "I guess I'll keep my room, and I'll show you to the other side of the house where you can stay."

She turned away, busying herself brushing three crumbs off the counter and into her cupped hand. Boone hadn't moved. She carried the crumbs over and brushed them into the sink, making a much bigger job out of it than it was. When she turned, he still hadn't moved.

"What?" she asked, like she didn't know. "You want to move into my room after all?" She wanted him there. With all her heart, she wanted him there. And maybe if he was, they could continue with the shallow relationship they'd started two weeks ago.

"No," he finally said.

She didn't allow her disappointment to show on her face. She couldn't allow him to see how much she wished she could believe he was different.

"Okay then. You can follow me." She moved toward the back hall and the steps,

"No."

Now she was the one who didn't understand. She tilted her head.

"I'll sleep in the barn."

"The barn?" She was shocked, and her voice showed it. "It's not heated. You'll freeze."

"Nah."

"How long are you going to stay there?"

One broad shoulder moved up. "I think we'll know when it's time for me to move."

She shivered. He didn't say "move into the house," and she felt like he was saying when he moved, it would be to her room, like he wasn't going to sleep anywhere in the house except with her.

"Okay." Her voice was once again calm. They could be friends. She actually wanted them to be friends. Boone was a nice guy. But he wasn't as perfect as what he was pretending to be. He couldn't be.

"There will probably be some folks coming to move their stuff out. And when I was out feeding with Bill this morning, there were still a few cattle and three horses that hadn't been taken."

"Okay." She wasn't sure what that had to do with her. Her domain was the house.

"You want to come out and look around with me?"

"I'm tired. I think I'll take a rest. I have some work to do in the office, too."

"What is it? I can help." He threw the containers in the trash and waited for her response.

It wasn't that she didn't want to be with him. She did. But... Why not? Why not enjoy his company? They were going to be together for a long time. So she'd just enjoy him, but she wouldn't let him get too close.

Some of the tension in her body eased as she made a solid decision. "Sweet Water, the town, usually has a Thanksgiving meal in the school gymnasium, but I volunteered to host it here at the ranch this year. I have a budget from the town, and I was going to throw in a little more and make it a nice event. I had everything redone this spring for the big ball, and I have ideas for fall décor as well as a meal plan plus seating arrangements—"

"Whoa." Boone put up his hand. "You love doing this."

"Well, yes. Who doesn't?"

He snorted. "You just got animated, and your cheeks got pink, and your eyes flashed, and you looked like a girl I met at a wedding not long ago. I danced with her for a bit."

He didn't even make an insinuation about what happened later, and she figured that was on purpose. So she went with it, tossing her head. "Really? You sound like you kind of like this girl."

"I did." He came a little closer, and she backed slowly toward the office door where all her folders and plans were. "But I never got her name."

"Well then, you need to work on your moves. You shouldn't have let her out of your sight without her name and number."

"Oh, my moves were good. I even taught her some. She was a fine dancer." He closed the distance as her back hit the office door.

She reached around for the knob. "Did you tell her?"

"I couldn't talk. All I wanted to do was watch her."

"That was your first mistake. You have to look in her eyes." She twisted the handle, and the door opened behind her. She stepped in, almost wishing she had the nerve to stand and see what Boone would do if she let him catch her. Of course, she wasn't moving so fast that he couldn't have gotten her if he wanted. Maybe he was just playing and wanted her to enjoy herself, too.

If her happy heartbeat and the fact that she couldn't stop smiling was any indication, he was successful.

She kind of thought that maybe when Boone was around, she'd better plan on having a good time.

Chapter 12

Boone was moving a wrapped hay bale from the stack beyond the corral when Roxane's son came walking up the lane. The bus must have dropped him off at the end of the lane. Of course it did. Just because it was Sweet Water Ranch didn't mean the bus treated the boy any differently than any of the other kids who got dropped off at the end of their lanes.

Boone figured the boy would go right in and see his mother after spending the weekend with Ryder and Nell, but the kid dropped his book bag off at the back walk and kept walking.

Maybe that was his regular routine. Boone kept rolling toward the corral gate. By the time he got there, the kid was standing by the fence, watching. He must have run pretty fast to cover twice the ground the skid loader had.

Boone didn't think too much of it and was getting ready to pull the latch to get out when a thought struck him.

Boone's dad had died when he was not much older than that kid, but he remembered how much he'd loved just being with his dad, dogging his footsteps and practically worshipping the ground he walked on. Just something in a boy that wanted the father in his life to pay attention to him.

Instead of gripping the latch, Boone met the boy's eyes and made a motion with his hand. The kid's eyes drew together before they brightened and a big smile cut through his face. He ran to the gate, unlatched it, and threw it open.

Boone drove through, checking behind him where, sure enough, the kid was shutting it. He grinned a little to himself. He'd wanted to get to know the kid. It wasn't going to be hard if the boy was this ea-

107

ger to help out. It'd just take patience on his part because it was always easier to do things oneself than it was to train someone else to help. Especially a kid. Boone had enough little brothers to know it could be a pain, but the rewards of having a boy work beside him as the kid turned into a man and actually became a real help would be worth the effort.

Always was.

Unless, of course, the dad died before he got to see the man his son had become.

He shoved those thoughts away. He hadn't thought of working with his dad in years. He'd gotten to work with his brothers all his life and in even closer quarters on the harvest crew he'd just left.

Now he had a ready-made family and a boy whose dad didn't seem to be too interested in him. It was funny how the Lord worked sometimes.

Boone stopped in front of the round bale holder and hopped out of the machine. Spencer had trailed along behind, warily eyeing the cattle that milled around.

Boone grinned. "They're big, but they're not gonna hurt ya. The bull's out in the pasture. These are just cows, and they'll never bother you unless they've just freshened. Sometimes you have a new mother that gets a little crazy protecting her offspring, but otherwise, you don't need to worry."

Spencer nodded, still not looking like he wanted to walk much closer.

Boone's mother would have flipped her brisket if he'd been out in the corral without changing his school clothes. But they were poor, and keeping school clothes nice to wear for an entire year and possibly more as hand-me-downs was an essential part of their budget. Spencer might not have the same constraints.

Boone gave quick consideration to the fact that Roxane might be mad at him for letting her son get dirty against the desire to include the boy in his work.

After three-quarters of a second, he jerked his head. "You have a pocketknife?" When he was that age, he wouldn't be caught dead without one. He and his brothers had sung specials in church with their weaponry strapped under their dress pants. Or, in some cases, clipped to their pockets and strapped to their chests. They'd had contests as to who could take the most knives to church and throwing contests afterwards as the adults lingered and talked.

Church wasn't boring when he was a boy.

Something told him Roxane might not approve.

Spencer shook his head, answering Boone's question and pulling him from his thoughts.

Boone pulled his knife out, flipped it open, and handed it to him, handle first. "We're gonna cut the plastic off this bale and cut the strings too. Think you can do it without a trip to the ER? Knife's sharp."

Spencer looked at it like he'd never held one before. Surely his mother didn't cut his steak for him. If the boy wasn't twelve, he was close to it.

"Cut a big X on the bottom of the bale." Boone pointed to the bottom end that was sticking out.

Spencer went over and slowly cut a small X, maybe four inches for each line.

Boone realized right away he should have shown the boy how to do it a few times before handing over the knife. His brothers had grown up outside, waddling around the corral in diapers that sagged in the dirt. So when they were handed a knife, they knew exactly what to do with it, even if they didn't always have the instincts to keep their fingers out of the way. He had a few scars on his own hands from the same lack of foresight. Funny how a little pain, a lot of blood, and a few stitches helped develop those capabilities.

Another thing he was pretty sure Roxane might have issues with. He could only picture her face if he led her son into the kitchen, dripping blood, and tried to explain it by saying he was "developing instincts."

Maybe he'd better make his spot in the barn a little more comfortable.

He didn't even want to think about that. He'd thought he was doing an okay job of talking to Roxane, but she'd left to take a nap yesterday, he hadn't seen her the rest of the day, and she hadn't been at breakfast this morning. Lunch had been quiet and strained.

He pulled his focus back to Spencer who had finished making the small cut. He could pull the plastic off the bale from the cut Spencer had made, but he didn't believe in working harder than he needed to. He also didn't want to take the knife back after he'd given it.

So he took his pointer finger and ran it from one side of the bale, through the small cut Spencer had made, and diagonally down to the opposite corner. Then he did the same thing from the other top side, making a much, much bigger X.

He lifted a brow at Spencer who had his nose wrinkled and his eyes narrowed. Boone liked his attitude.

The boy took the knife and followed, almost exactly, what Boone had shown him.

"Now, put it away." Boone had cut himself more than once from being in a hurry and not folding his knife back up before he started working, in this case, removing the plastic.

Spencer twisted the knife over and end to end, trying to figure out how to close it. Boone waited patiently. As patiently as the cows were waiting for their hay. Funny that with the knife in his hand, Spencer had forgotten all about being scared of the placid bovines.

Finally, the boy looked up, lines between his brows.

Boone took his thumb and rubbed it over the lever that released the metal, showing the motion. Spencer smiled, understanding brightening his face.

He took his own thumb and was about to push the lever when Boone stopped him. "Be careful with your fingers. You don't want them here with the blade coming down." He ran a finger along the bed where the blade would sink, protected, until the knife was opened again.

Spencer nodded solemnly, a very serious look on his face, like Boone had just entrusted him with the first half of the nuclear code. He carefully kept his fingers on the side of the knife as he moved the lever and folded it.

He handed it back to Boone.

"You have one?" Boone asked.

Spencer shook his head.

"Keep it." He let out a breath. "I took mine to school when I was your age, but it's a tool for work. It's not something to hurt people with, but you can use it for self-defense."

Spencer nodded, again solemnly. Boone hoped the boy always respected what he said as he was now doing, but he also hoped they could laugh and have fun together, too. It probably wasn't Spencer's fault that he didn't seem to know how to act around a man who paid attention to him.

Hopefully, Boone would have plenty of time to work on it.

He grabbed an end of the plastic and pulled, ripping the protective cover, looking at Spencer. He saw that as an invitation and started pulling the white wrap as well.

"Once I set it in the feeder, we'll be able to get the rest off and also pull the strings." He moved to get in the loader. "Stand back. I have to drop it, and sometimes it bounces. The bale's a lot heavier than the feeder, and you can never be sure what direction it's going to go."

Spencer looked around, his shoulders tensing as he saw the cattle towering over him. Boone watched until the boy lifted his head and balled his fists before running for the fence. There wasn't enough room in the loader for the boy to sit with him, or he'd have put him in with him.

He dropped the bale in and got out immediately, motioning for Spencer to come over. "Gonna need your knife."

After a brief hesitation and a look at the cows, Spencer ran straight to Boone, a happy grin on his face. The boy felt good to be needed. Roxane might be upset about Boone giving him a knife, especially without asking her first—after all, the kid was hers—but at that moment, Boone didn't care.

He showed him where the strings were and how to cut them. The cows were nosing in, hunger overcoming their natural inclination to stand back from the humans. Boone appreciated the people who had handled these cattle before. They weren't pets, but they weren't so wild as to be crazy and dangerous.

"We have to make sure we get every string out. If one of these ladies gets one in her stomach, it's gonna give her a bellyache."

Spencer laughed. "She'd get to stay home from school."

Boone chuckled. "I suppose." He pulled plastic in one hand and string in another. "But it's our job to take care of them. Not only does the righteous man regard the life of his beast, but they also represent our livelihood. It's wrong and wasteful to not take as good care of them as we can."

Spencer nodded, like he actually understood. Whether he did or not, Boone wasn't sure, but again, there should be plenty of time to teach life lessons as they worked together through the years. Years that would fly away as fast as the years of his own youth had. For some reason, the Lord had given him time with this boy, and he'd do the best he could to teach him while he had him.

Hopefully Roxane would be okay with it.

"I'll take this junk," Boone said, indicating the strings and plastic wrap, "if you want to bring the skid loader out of the corral."

Spencer's eyes got huge, golf ball size.

"I don't know how to drive it," he practically whispered.

"You play video games, right?"

Spencer nodded.

"It's probably about the same." Except a wrong turn on a video game wouldn't take down half the corral fence. "I'll show you. Hop in."

The skid loader rumbled on a low idle. Spencer crawled in, pulling and tugging on the safety harness until he got it down over him.

Boone draped the wrap and strings over the grippers and stood on the front of the loader. He could probably run it backward, but there was no need. The boy couldn't hurt anything but the fence, and if he knocked that down, they'd move the cows and he and Boone would fix it. It'd be another good lesson.

"When your safety harness goes up, everything stops." Boone patted the bulky shoulder restraint that surrounded Spencer, who nodded. He pointed out the controls, moving them a little as he explained them to show what they did. "Give me a second to jump off and get the garbage, and I'll open the gate for you. If you feel comfortable, you can take it the whole way over to the shed. I'd better park it for today, and I think we should go in and see your mom. Maybe you can practice driving later this evening." Boone looked the boy in the eye. "You have homework?"

Spencer nodded, a bit sheepishly.

He laughed. "Let's talk to your mom about what you're allowed to do." He hopped off, grabbing his junk, and started toward the gate. His step only faltered slightly when he realized Roxane was standing on the other side of it, her arms crossed over her chest. She wasn't smiling.

His heart stumbled just a bit. The wind caught her hair and blew it away from her face, showcasing her high cheekbones and the intelligence in her eyes. Eyes that were narrowed slightly as she looked at him. Then her gaze swept back to her son, and worry tightened her features. He thought she might be biting the insides of her cheeks, too.

He turned, looking back over his shoulder. The skid loader bumped and jumped as Spencer jerked at the controls. Typical.

He brushed a cow with the ends of the hay grippers as he turned. The large black animal barely noticed as she continued to burrow her nose in the hay. After a bunch more wobbles and bumps, the boy finally got the machine turned and started moving slowly toward the gate. With the machine still on a low idle, he wasn't going anywhere fast.

Boone turned back around to face Roxane and moved to the gate. She didn't look angry, exactly. She did, however, look beautiful. Classy. With an aristocratic turn to her nose and a slight tilt to her head. It made him feel like she was every inch a socialite and he was exactly what he was, a dirt-poor cowboy who'd married into money and was playing at ranching.

He didn't resent her, not even a little, but he did feel like maybe he belonged in the barn.

He also felt like he never wanted to take his eyes off her.

Holding the trash with one hand and an elbow, he unhooked the gate and pushed it out. Roxane moved back.

Boone held the gate so it didn't swing and turned back to watch Spencer. "He's doing fine," he said to the woman glaring at his back.

"He hasn't died. Yet. I consider that a win." Her voice held some frost, but he didn't detect much anger.

"I told him he could take it to the shed and I'd park it. We were coming in then, to talk to you." He wasn't afraid of her. But he didn't turn to look at her, either.

"Oh? I thought maybe you two were planning on staying out here all night."

"I'll stay here, and you can meet him when he gets off. See what he says we were going to do."

"I believe you. I'm just not real happy to see such a little boy operating such a dangerous piece of equipment. Alone."

"There's not enough room for both of us in there. The throttle's down low, and it'll stop as soon as he stops pressing forward." He finally turned. It was always hard for him to look at her without wanting to touch her. And he hated that she wasn't exactly happy with him. "When I first started driving our skid loader when I was a kid, I was so little I didn't weigh enough to trip the safety switch on the seat and my dad had to hotwire it to keep the thing running while I drove."

"I stood on the auction block and allowed myself to be sold to the highest bidder. Just because it happened to me doesn't mean that I want it for my kids. Or that they should have it."

The skid loader drove by them, Spencer in the seat with a smile that reached to the moon and back. Boone wasn't in a big hurry to shut the gate behind him since all the cattle were crowded up around the feeder. He waited until he didn't have to yell, his chest hurting.

"I wasn't saying that because I did it, he should too. I was saying it is a big machine, and he is young, but it won't hurt him. As for you, it might be a little too early to draw a definite conclusion, but I think having the guts to keep your word and stand on that auction block showed a strength of character that most people don't possess. As for how it turned out, I guess you'll have to see about it."

He didn't know what else to say. He was pretty darn pleased with how it turned out. Couldn't be much happier, really.

She blew out a breath and turned slightly away from him, watching her son as he moved the machine slowly across the yard toward the shed. "I'm sorry. My words were a little harsher than I intended. It scares me to see him in that thing."

Boone appreciated the apology. He supposed he ought to tell her so, but his insides still felt twisted and irritated by her insinuation that being married to him was a bad thing.

Like she knew it, she turned. "The auction turned out better than I could have hoped. And I appreciate you spending time with my son." She lifted her chin but didn't meet his eyes. "I also trust you to make sure he doesn't get hurt, and I'll try to keep my mouth shut."

She made to turn, but he touched her arm. She stopped, staring at the line of the horizon in the distance.

"I can't guarantee that he won't get hurt."

Her mouth pressed tight together.

"This isn't the city where we all walk around in our safe little bubbles with pillows strapped to our backsides, warning labels on matches telling us they're hot, and lawsuits for broken fingernails and hot coffee flying around with abandon. You can't survive out here without living the danger."

"There are no bubbles and pillows, and living in the city can be dangerous, too." She crossed her arms over her chest.

"You'd be the expert on that, so I stand corrected. Seems to me the bad guys have the advantage in the city, so I try to stay away."

Her brow furrowed, and she didn't seem to understand. He didn't bother to explain that he would never be comfortable somewhere that didn't allow a man to defend himself, his wife, and his children with whatever weaponry necessary. It was one more thing they disagreed on, and he'd already had enough disappointment for one day.

He shoved his hat down farther on his head and pushed the gate closed. "I told Spencer I'd park it. We were planning on coming in and talking to you. That suit you?" Latching the gate as he spoke, he didn't bother to turn around.

"Yes." She turned and walked gracefully to the house, her stride confident, her bearing proud. He felt incompetent and off-kilter around her. Not that she was better than him, just living in a different world. One where social graces mattered and money talked. Where men spent their days under artificial lights in boardrooms, punching buttons on keyboards and talking about the latest fashion trends.

Nothing wrong with that, but it wasn't him and never would be. It hurt to think that was what she wanted.

Chapter 13

Spencer and Boone walked into the kitchen five minutes later. Roxane finally had her heart and breathing back under control. Her heart had felt like it jumped up and grabbed her tonsils in a death grip when she saw her little boy in that machine. And Boone was walking away from him like it wasn't dangerous at all. Like he couldn't be hurt.

Of course he'd been right. Spencer was fine.

Boone had also been right about Spencer needing to do these things. And Roxane was thrilled that Boone was taking the time to work with him.

But she hadn't said that.

Instead she got all haughty and started arguing about city life versus living on a ranch. Of course they were different. And from the way Boone looked, he'd gotten the impression she thought she was better than he was, like she was insulting him and his way of life.

But she'd already apologized once. It hadn't been enough to ease the sting from his features.

Mrs. Sprouse had supper in the oven and had left for the day, but she'd set a plate of meat and cheese and veggies with dip in the fridge. Roxane got it out and uncovered it. She'd spent a good bit of her day planning the Thanksgiving meal that the ranch was hosting—something she loved. But she kind of wished she hadn't felt so restless and...lonely. Maybe it was because she was now married, even if it hadn't been a love match, but maybe she felt like she was missing out because it wasn't.

Or maybe she just didn't like the tension that seemed to have settled between them. They'd had a nice conversation Sunday. She thought they'd cleared some things up, but lunch had been strained, and now...maybe she messed everything up by being upset.

She loved that he was working with Spencer, and she wanted to be friends with Boone. More than friends, if she were honest.

So, she was going to be nice. Maybe she could flirt.

Boone and Spencer had washed their hands when she turned from the fridge with the tray, smiling as sweetly as she could.

Boone's eyes widened, then they narrowed, and he looked around the kitchen, finally settling his eyes on the tray she held, suspicion entering his expression.

Great.

She'd gotten to the point that when she smiled at him, he became suspicious.

Lovely.

What a mess she'd made of everything.

Well, she didn't know what to do about Boone, but she could talk to her son at least.

"How was your day at school?" she asked, her voice pleasant.

"Good." Spencer eyed the tray as she set it on the bar.

"Anything happen?" They had this same conversation every day.

"No."

Boone hadn't said anything, and she really didn't expect him to. He hadn't planted himself on a barstool like Spencer had, either. Like he wasn't entirely sure he was welcome.

She looked at him. "You can help yourself, too."

"Thanks," he said, closing the distance between himself and the bar. "I might be a little late for supper if I'm gonna go get the tractor and bring the grain drill back."

"Can I go too? Can I help? I could drive the skid loader if you need it!" Spencer's mouth was full. Roxane bit her tongue over the reprimand to not talk. She'd just been complaining that he didn't.

Boone put a hand on the bar. "We need to talk to your mother about what you're allowed to do. She also asked you about your day, and she probably wants more than two words."

Spencer looked at him, chewing, like he couldn't figure out what to say. Roxane opened her mouth, but Boone beat her to it.

"Like this: after I fed the stock this morning, I worried a little about my wife because she wasn't down for breakfast. I hit my thumb with a hammer while I was pounding in a nail in the tack room," he flashed a grin at her, and she got a little distracted by his dimple, "and God was listening, so all I said was 'ouch,' only in a much, much louder voice."

Spencer was craning his head, trying to see the nail, so Boone held it up. Roxie's stomach pinched.

"Cracked the nail, but it'll be as good as new next year this time."

"You're not going to put anything on it?" Roxie shook her head and walked to the cupboard. "Never mind."

The bandages were right where they were supposed to be, so she got one out and went back over.

"She wants to know about your day, bub. So you think of the high-lights and give her a couple of sentences. It makes her happy."

"But she's putting a bandage on you now, and she wouldn't have if you hadn't said anything."

"Hey, look on the bright side, it could be pink."

"Pink?"

"Sure. My little sister had pink bandages." He grunted, his dimple appearing again. "Maybe she still does. She's pretty girly."

"There's nothing wrong with pink. With your complexion, it would actually look good on you." Roxie tried to ease her serious expression. She should have asked him if he wanted a bandage. She had a tendency to be a drill sergeant. It came out more when she was nervous. She tried to ease the sting out of her voice. "But that blue brings out your eyes."

Those eyes narrowed almost immediately. Yeah. Too much a drill sergeant and she ran people off; too much the other direction and she made him suspicious.

"I didn't bang my hand with a hammer, but I did tackle Dalton on the playground."

Roxie couldn't stop her gasp.

She glanced at Boone. He didn't seem overly concerned. She tried to temper her reaction. She clasped her hands together on the bar top.

"But that was only because he threw a worm on Emma."

Boone picked up a piece of meat. "Are we going to get a call from your teacher?"

Spencer shrugged. "I don't think so. They made me sit down, but Emma came over and told them what happened, so then Dalton got in trouble, too."

"Did they let you up?" Roxie couldn't stop herself from asking.

"Not until recess was over." Her son hopped off his chair and grabbed a glass, filling it with water from the sink.

"Sounds good to me. If she's your friend, you have to stick up for her, but you have to face the consequences." Boone lifted one big shoulder before putting the meat in his mouth.

"What?" Roxie stared. "It's not okay to 'tackle' people just because you have a disagreement with them."

Boone eyed her but didn't say anything.

Spencer took a long drink from his glass. "I'm going up to change my clothes." He ran out of the kitchen.

Roxie was right. She knew she was. Of course she was. Kids shouldn't tackle other kids.

She wanted Boone to admit it.

But she clamped her teeth together and forced her brain to work. Boone was an honorable man. She was sure of it. She'd seen it. If he said that things worked out okay, maybe she needed to think about it before demanding she was right.

"How could that be okay?" she managed to ask without her voice sounding shrill. So far, so good.

He chewed silently, studying her like he thought pretty much anything he said was going to make her mad. She determined it wouldn't.

Finally, when she wasn't sure he was even going to answer, he said, "Maybe we disagree on this, but I feel a man's job is to protect his wife and family. His home. His town, his country. I'm not saying it's pretty, and I'm not saying it doesn't hurt. There are consequences. Still, Spencer's got that instinct, and he used it today on the playground. I'm not going to pretend that a man's instinct to protect, and to do it in an aggressive, physical way, is somehow wrong or abnormal." One lip pulled up. "He was punished for it, so he saw there were consequences."

Her hands squeezed together. "I just don't want him to grow up to be a jerk." She didn't say, *like his father*, but she wanted to.

Actually, she wouldn't mind at all if Spencer grew up to be just like Boone.

"I don't think you have to worry about that, Roxie."

She loved being called Roxane, but somehow when he said "Roxie," it sounded different than the way everyone else said it. Like a caress.

She looked down. His large hand lay on the bar top, just inches away from hers. The differences were striking. Even with the bandage on his thumb, his hand looked masculine and tough. The kind of hand that actually could defend and protect her. Attached to a man who actually would do such things.

She had to admit the differences between them were really what drew her. He wasn't better, just different, and in a good, right way. She wouldn't want her son to turn out any differently. But if she had a daughter, she wouldn't want that for her. Did that mean she would parent her children differently?

Wasn't that wrong?

Shouldn't she give her son baby dolls and her daughter trucks?

She allowed her eyes to drag up Boone's torso, trying to imagine him playing with dolls. The image was kind of cute, but she wouldn't be attracted to him if that were his preference.

She also wouldn't be attracted to him if he just meekly allowed her to run all over him.

And was she now admitting that she was attracted to him?

"I don't know what you're thinking," he said, leaning over the counter and lowering his voice, "but I like that look."

Her grin flashed before she could help it. Busted. But she wasn't trying to pretend she wasn't attracted to her husband, right?

"I was just thinking about how different we are and...how I liked it."

His lips curved up even farther. "Is this a good time to tell you I gave Spencer my pocketknife?"

His voice had gotten husky and low, and she'd gotten a little lost in those deep blue eyes, so it took her about two seconds to actually hear what he said.

She gasped and pulled back. Her mouth moved up and down, faster than her brain could function, but thankfully no sound came out.

Managing to close her mouth, she pressed her lips together tight and pinched the bridge of her nose.

"You gave him a pocketknife?" she asked slowly.

"I gave him my pocketknife. A boy needs one. I can hardly take it back, so you'll have to if you don't want him to have it."

"Why does a boy need a pocketknife?" She tilted her head and looked at him. Did she want her son to turn out like him?

His lip twitched, and she thought he might be going to give her a sarcastic answer, but he straightened. "I use it all the time. We just used it outside to cut a hay bale open. Fix a hose, impromptu screwdriver, sharpen a pencil, dig a splinter out."

"That's not sanitary."

"Hasn't killed me yet."

"Okay. I see. He can't take it to school."

"Then maybe he ought not to be in school. You can't send a kid to school with no way to defend himself."

She stared at him, knowing he wasn't suggesting her son get into a knife fight at school but not knowing exactly what he meant.

"Did you talk to her?" Spencer bounced in, completely changed, and grabbed crackers and meat.

"Not about that." He looked over the counter at Roxie, and she could hardly believe they were still talking, considering how radical his ideas were.

"About what?" she asked, determined not to fight in front of her son.

"When Spencer gets home from school, can he work with me until dark then do his schoolwork when we come in?" Boone ran a hand through his hair. "What exactly is he allowed to do?"

Roxie pursed her lips. She wanted to say his schoolwork needed to be done first. That her son shouldn't be doing anything dangerous or anything where he could get hurt. That she'd take care of him.

But those weren't the words that came out of her mouth. "I guess I don't know what your schedule is going to be. Whatever you decide. I only think he needs to get his schoolwork done, take a shower, and be in bed no later than ten."

She tilted her head and looked at Boone as she finished speaking, so she couldn't miss the drop of his chin.

"He might get dirty."

"That's why we have showers."

"He might be out from the time he comes home until dark."

"As long as he gets his schoolwork done."

"He might get hurt."

"If he does, you'll have to deal with a hysterical wife, too."

"One of us will have to hold it together."

"You."

"You sure?" He seemed to search her eyes.

"Yes."

Spencer jumped up. "Yes!" he screeched, running around the counter and throwing his arms around Roxie.

Her little boy was growing up, and maybe she held him a little tighter than she needed to, looking over his head and into the true eyes of the cowboy who'd stood up on Saturday night, claimed her, and married her.

Spencer yanked away, hurrying toward Boone. "You ready? Can I drive the skid loader? Huh?"

"Maybe your mother will come with us?" Boone looked over his head at her, and her chest constricted. His lips tilted up just a tad, but he looked like he actually wanted her. What would she do? She couldn't work outside. She didn't have the first clue of what to do.

"Yeah, Mom. You come too." Spencer looked eager.

"I'm not really dressed for it," she said, not used to being unsure.

Boone seemed to realize she'd really like to go but was having uncharacteristic difficulty making a decision. He held his hand out, over the counter. "Come with us," he said softly.

She looked at his hand then at the face of her son. Maybe they could really be a family. But she would need to give some, too.

She took a breath and put her hand in his. "Okay." She blew her breath out and pulled her hand away. "I need to take the casserole out of the oven."

Chapter 14

Boone couldn't have been more shocked when Roxane agreed to come with him. He had to admit he really liked the idea. It was only Monday; he'd only been married for two days, but it was hard to remember it was all real. He really had a wife. Sweet Water was his responsibility. There was a child coming and one already here.

Roxane took the casserole out of the oven while Spencer and he exchanged a look. Spencer gave a grin and a shrug. Boone gave a cocky wink. Why not? He was feeling pretty good. Roxane must not hate him too bad if she just agreed to come out and work with him for an hour before dark.

She set the casserole on the stove and put the mitts beside it.

He held out his hand again. This time, she didn't hesitate as long before she grabbed it. He allowed their clasped hands to swing between them as they walked through the office and out the back door, Spencer running ahead.

"Can I practice in the skid loader? Can I? Please?" He practically danced up the walk backward as he asked.

"Let's see where Bill is. I need to head out along the fence line and check the stock in the back pasture. I need to bring the grain drill back, and I'll have to take a tractor. If Bill's around, he might be able to keep an eye on you."

"I'll go find him." Spencer took off running.

Boone suspected Bill wouldn't mind keeping an eye on Spencer, but Boone would definitely be talking to him first.

Roxane's hand had tightened in his. Then, like she was forcing it, it loosened.

He found Bill where he was changing the oil in the small tractor they used to mow. He was fine with keeping an eye on Spencer.

As they walked away from Spencer who was riding the skid loader, Roxane allowed her hand to stay in his. Boone looked down at her, a few butterflies in his stomach now that they were alone again, without the buffer of Spencer between them.

Boone pulled Roxane around the barn to where the midsize tractor that he'd bring the grain drill back with was parked. It had an enclosed cab and a small seat for a rider, which would probably make Roxane more comfortable than the smaller tractor he'd been planning on using, where she would have had to sit on the fender.

"Are you feeling okay?" he asked, unsure how the whole pregnancy sickness thing worked. He should look it up so he'd know a little better what to expect.

"Yes. I'm fine," she said, her voice never wavering. "I think the auction and the stress from that just really took a toll."

His brow wrinkled. It probably had. If he'd known about the pregnancy, he could have done a better job of shielding her from it.

Maybe she wouldn't have let him.

"I'm sorry," he finally said, as they made the turn and headed toward the equipment shed.

"It's not your fault."

He didn't say anything. No point in arguing. She already knew he wanted to protect her. Thought it was his job.

"What are we doing?" she asked.

Maybe her voice had a little forced happiness in it. He wasn't sure.

"When the wheat was harvested, they planted a cover crop, probably rye, but I didn't ask Bill. They left the grain drill out in the last field they did, and we're going out to pick it up."

"Oh." She looked off in the distance as the sun settled lower in the sky. "Is that it for the year?"

He grunted a little laugh. "No. Not at all. I'm gonna check the weather, but if the rain is going to hold off for a couple of days, I'm going to mow hay tomorrow."

"Okay."

He didn't want to, but he let go of her hand to open the big sliding door so he could drive the tractor out of the shed. "It's pretty late in the year, and it won't dry, but I can bale it wet and wrap it. Cows will love it this winter."

"Why won't it dry? If it's not raining?"

She seemed really interested. It made him smile. "Well, first of all, it gets pretty cold at night and takes a while to warm up. Then, days are getting shorter and the angle of the sun is more toward the horizon. It's not impossible, but it takes longer, and you run the risk of rain, plus hay quality goes down."

"I see."

She looked around the equipment shed like she'd never been in it before. Maybe she hadn't.

He nodded at the enclosed cab tractor in front of them. "This is the one we're taking. I'll open the door, and you can climb up."

He reached up and pulled the door open with a hiss. Roxane, looking every inch the aristocratic lady, gave the steps up an uncertain glance before she put her nose in the air and took ahold of the handle. He held his hand out, in case she wanted to grab it too.

He smiled when she did.

She climbed in easily and settled in her seat.

He climbed into his, but before he started it, he asked, "You want to drive?"

A startled grunt burst from her lips. "Not today," she said, but she was smiling. He thought it made her feel good that he'd ask, and he was glad he did.

He started the tractor, glad he got to do something with her where he felt like he was in his element. Dancing, he was okay at. Romancing women, not at all, and Roxane knew it. Knowing what to say to his wife was something else he wasn't good at, and figuring out what she was thinking felt impossible.

But he could drive a tractor, and he could do it with confidence.

"You seem like you feel at home on the ranch." Roxane sat straight and looked around. He liked that she still wanted to talk to him; maybe he liked it more that she'd noticed him and thought him competent.

"I grew up on a ranch not far from here, plus I've worked here a few times, haying and harvesting, planting. Bill's been good, too, but this isn't totally new to me." He pulled the tractor out and drove slowly along the back road before turning and heading down the field road. "What about you? Weren't you here some when you were younger?"

"I was, but I never helped out much outside. Our mom was pretty protective."

He wanted to know more about her. The things that he might have found out if they'd been dating. All the things he'd missed when they danced and went too far. He didn't know if it were possible to back up and do things right, but he wanted to try.

"Were you here much?" he asked, hoping he didn't push too hard too fast and scare her away.

"A few summers. Ryder was here longer. Mom couldn't handle the remoteness, but our uncle insisted, even though we didn't see him much."

"The same uncle that made the will?"

She laughed without humor. "Yep. That one."

They were going slow enough that to pretend he needed to keep his eyes glued on the straight, flat road was completely unbelievable. Still, he didn't look at her when he asked, "So what'd you do the rest of the year?"

Her head tilted, and her eyes narrowed, like she was trying to figure out why he asked.

He put a hand up in innocence. "You don't have to answer. I'm asking because I'm curious." Now he did turn his head and meet her gaze head-on. "I know we're married. I know it was forced. But you have to know...I like you. I'd love to know everything you are willing to tell me about yourself."

"I doubt that." There was a dry note in her voice. She didn't respond to his admission that he liked her. "Like" wasn't really the emotion he probably felt, anyway. He wasn't sure exactly what pulled him to her with the same kind of force windmill blades were compelled to spin in front of a wind. But it wasn't "like" the way he liked any of his friends or family. It was definitely something stronger and deeper.

"Try me."

"Someone like you doesn't really know what it's like to have a past you wished you didn't have."

Someone like him.

His hands tightened on the steering wheel of the tractor, and he stared at the road without seeing it. She put distance between them with those words.

Almost the implication that he was "good" so he didn't have struggles or pain or regrets. That his life had been easy and clear, and sure, maybe his dad had died, but nothing else bad had happened.

He'd met that attitude before. "You know, that's one of two prevalent attitudes I get from people."

He turned down between two fields that had already been planted in rye. Little green sprouts had turned the brown earth a delicate green, pretty against the big, deep blue North Dakota sky.

"Oh?" she said. "You sound annoyed. I really meant it as a compliment."

He pulled a lip back. Yeah, he was annoyed. But there really was no reason for it. She was calling it as she saw it. Just because she saw it wrong didn't make her unkind.

He decided to drop it. She would never understand that trying to be what he'd tried to be, with the world the way it was, felt like being a tennis ball floating in the middle of the Atlantic Ocean with occasional ocean liners cruising by, their parties of people pointing at him and laughing, mostly.

"If you don't want to tell me about it, that's fine," he finally said. He didn't really want to tell her how mistaken she was, either.

She shrugged. "I was young, and I was rich. I didn't live quite like you see on TV, but the opportunities were there, and I didn't turn them down." She spoke softly and stared out the window in front of them, acres upon acres of North Dakota flatland stretching out and meeting the sky. Old friends.

And he'd been a part of that for years. Not always in North Dakota, but in his travels on the harvest crew, he'd looked out plenty of windows, both on the road and in the fields, and seen nothing but the fertile fields of America, stretching out to meet the sky. Fields filled with ripened grain. Grown by hardworking American farmers and ready to feed the country and the world. He'd always been proud to be a part of it.

Now, he'd married into his own spread.

But his wife only saw what she wanted to on the surface.

"We dated off and on through college. Eventually we had a long enough 'on' time to plan a wedding and get married. He came from my social circles, and I thought after we got married he'd quit playing the field. In hindsight, it's stupid to think a man's going to change just because he got married. If he was a player before, he's going to keep being a player." Her fingers picked at the stitching on the seat.

He didn't think she even noticed.

He wanted to joke about being a better husband than Bryan, but he didn't think she'd laugh about it. He was trying to woo her, not drive her away. But he wasn't used to living life so seriously. Living with the harvest crew had taught him that. They wouldn't let him be sorry for himself or not laugh at life.

"So all I have to do to be a better husband than Bryan is stay home at night?" He lifted a brow.

Her lips pursed. "And during the day."

"Can I go somewhere if I take you with me?"

"I'm not watching you flirt with other women."

"I'd have to learn how first. I don't think I want to waste the time unless I can use my new skills on you." He eyed her out of the corner of his eye before pulling the tractor in ahead of the planter and easing the clutch in.

"You can flirt," she scoffed.

"Cannot," he said automatically, watching carefully to be sure he lined the hitches up.

"You were flirting the day of Clay's wedding." Her mouth clamped closed like that was a subject she didn't want to talk about.

It was done. They might as well admit it was part of their history. Maybe they could laugh about that someday. She could probably laugh about it now. He still felt a little sensitive about it.

"Then maybe it's something that comes naturally." He stopped the tractor and set the brake. "I didn't mean to flirt." His lip kicked up in a half grin. "I just liked you."

Her mouth made an "o." He pushed up and slipped past her, opening the door. "You coming down?" he asked, one foot on the top step before he stopped abruptly and turned. Maybe he could flirt.

He pushed his cowboy hat down on his head and allowed one side of his mouth to tilt. In a low voice with just a hint of humor, he said, "You wanna meet me behind the tractor?"

She blinked twice, and her eyes flew to his, surprise and confusion giving way to a little smile of her own. It made his heart trip.

She lifted her nose and looked down it. His crooked grin wanted to straighten into a full-on smile.

"I don't know, stranger. What are you thinking we're going to do back there?"

"Hook up."

Her mouth dropped, and it wasn't just pretend. "I can't believe you would suggest that here, in front of God and everyone."

He did laugh at that because it was just God, there was no "everyone." But he sobered quickly, moving down the ladder and shaking his head. "I was talking about the grain drill. I was going to hook the grain drill up to the tractor." He grinned again. "You better get your butt down here and learn how to do it. Next time, I'll send you out to get it by yourself while I take a nap."

"Ha. You won't be napping. You'll be eating your way through my refrigerator."

He snort-laughed.

She put her hand in his. She paused, and their eyes met. His smile faded. Her fake-haughty look fell, replaced by confusion then awareness.

Her chest lifted, and she stepped down. He didn't back up. And he didn't let go of her hand. He supposed flirting implied words, but some things were better without words.

He put his free hand on her waist, just resting there.

She touched her tongue to her bottom lip, and he watched it, not even trying to pretend he wasn't. Her breath hitched. His did too, but his lip curved up as well. He met her eyes before dropping his gaze back to her lip, shiny now. She saw what he was looking at, and he didn't care. Her mouth parted, almost in surprise, and her breath huffed out.

Flirting without words.

He could do it. It was fun, actually. Except he didn't want to turn away and get back to work. He wanted to pull her closer and do more than flirt.

"You have that grain drill hooked up yet?" he asked, his voice low with a note of humor, laughing at himself because he was standing here staring at his wife's lips rather than doing his job. No wonder Adam ate the fruit. Keeping the garden wouldn't have been half as fun if Eve had gotten kicked out and he hadn't.

Right now, he was a pure son of Adam because he'd eat the fruit too. Anything to keep Roxane with him.

"I've got a feeling I'm not going to want to work without you again."

"That's funny," she said, in the same low, humorous tone he used. "Because I was just thinking I might want to put my boots on tomorrow and be your boss."

His fingers flexed on her waist. "Sounds fun. Maybe you can sit on my lap and teach me how to drive."

She rolled her eyes and pushed at his chest. He moved back without resistance, his hand sliding down. "Go hitch that thing up. Bill is going to think we got sidetracked out here."

"Oh? Is that what it's called? Sidetracked?" He walked back to the hitch, grinning, his heart beating hard and his breath coming fast. It probably wasn't smart to not be focused on his work. He'd have to remember no flirting when he was doing more than moving equipment from one location to another.

Her voice had been light, but she watched him intently. He had no doubt she'd be able to do it herself next time. Most of the stuff he did wasn't rocket science. Just long hours.

He dropped the pin in and straightened. "Got that?"

Maybe he'd thought she looked out of place out here, with her tailored pants and her delicate skin. Funny, maybe she did look that way, but he felt like she belonged right where she was. Whether it was a part of the North Dakota prairie or, more likely, right beside him. The rightness settled down deep. He breathed into it, trying to keep his mouth from saying things she wasn't ready to hear yet.

"You can take your nap next time. I'm on it." She flipped her hair over her shoulder.

"You drive me home, and I'll believe it." He balled his fist to keep from touching a strand that caught on the corner of her mouth.

One eye closed slightly, like she was considering his challenge. He loved her fearless attitude.

"Sure. I'll drive home, but when you come in for the night, you're helping me make decorations for the Thanksgiving dinner."

"If you want me to," he said easily, knowing he didn't have an artistic bone in his body. She'd figure that out soon enough, and he'd get fired. 'Course, if she drove the tractor into the barn, they'd get it out and fix the hole, and he'd tell her to keep practicing. Maybe decorating was the same way. She'd make him keep practicing until he got it. Unless he cut a finger off. Maybe he'd be excused at that point. He'd have to think on it.

Chapter 15

They had settled into a routine after those first tough days. Roxie wasn't sure whether to be happy about that or not so thrilled.

If Boone was doing something where she could ride along safely or even help, that's what they did. When Spencer got home, they'd all three work together. After supper, when it was dark, Boone really did help her with the Thanksgiving dinner planning and preparation.

He'd have them both laughing, entertaining them with stories from the last eight or so years that he'd spent on the harvest crew or pranks he and his brothers played when they were teens growing up. Almost every night, Roxane laughed so hard her eyes watered and her stomach hurt. Boone was an easy man to like.

Of course, he'd kept on teasing her, and she'd continued to respond in kind. Flirting, really. Sometimes without words.

She suspected that she more than "liked" Boone.

But when she sent Spencer up to get ready for bed, Boone left to shower and sleep in the barn.

She wasn't sure why, exactly, and she also wasn't sure what needed to happen to get him to stay.

It was getting well below freezing on these late November nights. Maybe tonight he'd stay in.

Spencer was spending the weekend with Vinton, and Boone had suggested they go in to the diner to eat.

It was Friday night, and she had a date with her husband. That hadn't happened in a long time. She quit early to get ready. He showered in the barn.

When she came down the stairs, after changing her outfit three times and finally settling on jeans—that thankfully still fit—and a loose white blouse over a green tank, he was standing in the kitchen doorway with his hands in his pockets, his shoulder leaning on the doorjamb.

He wore dark blue jeans, a black button-down, along with boots. His hat lay on the bar behind him, and his hair was just long enough to be slicked to the side.

She put a hand over her stomach where butterflies were suddenly doing jumping jacks.

Immediately his brow furrowed, and he straightened. "Are you okay? The baby's okay?"

They'd gone to the clinic in Rockerton together, and she couldn't get the look of wonder he'd had on his face out of her mind. There was no question he'd been enraptured by hearing the heartbeat of their child.

She dropped her hand. "Fine. Everything's fine." She still got sick occasionally during the day, but it was mostly confined to morning, and she didn't want anything to keep her from going out with her husband tonight.

"You look amazing," he said.

It wasn't so much his words but more his tone and the look on his face that made her heart swell. It didn't take a huge bunch of flowery compliments but three simple words from a sincere heart. The humor that crinkled his eyes and turned his lips up so easily while they worked was absent.

"Thank you," she said softly.

He took another three breaths while they stood and stared at each other before he stepped forward and held his hand out.

She took it, and they got in his truck and drove to town without the relaxed banter that had become their norm.

Maybe his silence didn't mean anything, but Boone was an easy talker, unlike some men she'd been around, and he wasn't ever this quiet. Finally, when they were almost to Sweet Water, she couldn't take it any longer. "Why are you so quiet?"

His grin was a little self-effacing as he glanced over at her. She was just happy to see his smile.

"Confidence isn't something I typically have a problem with, but you're so poised and elegant, I feel like an awkward kid with junior high stamped on my forehead." He gave her another glance, this one devoid of humor. "I think that is probably an accurate assessment of me with you."

He slowed as the buildings of Sweet Water sprang up on either side of them.

She wanted to reassure him, but she wasn't sure what to say. She couldn't make herself be different than what she was. And if he were referring to their intimate encounter, he had been awkward but in an adorably sweet and wonderful way that had only made everything better for her, because she knew it meant something to him. Unlike Bryan who maybe knew all the words to say and moves to make but only because he'd practiced them on a multitude of other women. He'd been a playboy. He still was a playboy.

She'd take Boone's sincere admiration any day.

He pulled into a spot not far from the diner, shutting off the truck and looking over at her. "I'll get your door."

He jumped out and strode around. She fiddled with her purse strap, wondering why she was nervous. This was Boone; they'd been working together for weeks. There was no reason for nerves.

He opened her door, and she got out. He took her hand, his brow raised just slightly as he did, looking at her as though checking to see if it was okay. Her lips turned up, then her stomach flipped as he raised their joined hands to his lips and kissed her knuckle.

He grinned at the surprised look on her face, but she was too busy trying to get her stomach under control to work on her facial expression, too.

Instead of opening the diner door, he stopped and tugged her closer, leaning his head down and whispering in her ear, "When you look at me like that, it makes me feel like it might not matter that I'm junior high and you're way out of my league."

She closed her eyes at the rumble in her ear and the spicy scent that teased her nose. She forced her throat to work. "You're right. It doesn't matter." Her voice was husky and soft, and she didn't have to touch him to know that he shuddered. She didn't have the brainpower to argue that experience didn't matter nor to explain to him what did. Another day.

"I want to kiss you later."

He hadn't moved. Hadn't touched her other than their joined hands, but his words stroked through her and made her shiver. They weren't the most romantic words in the world, but there could be no doubt he meant them and wanted her.

She tilted her head so the stubble on his cheek just grazed her skin. "I'll hold you to that."

His hand squeezed, but otherwise they didn't move for several seconds.

"Suddenly eating doesn't seem as important as it's always been, but we'd better get out of the doorway." He gave a short laugh as he pulled away. "Didn't think there was too much that would make me think that skipping a meal was a good idea."

He pulled the door open and allowed her to step inside first, their hands still joined.

Almost immediately, she noticed the change in him.

It wasn't a change like the quietness of the ride here but a tension that stiffened his muscles and changed the air around him.

Roxane looked around. The diner was as busy as she'd ever seen it, with most of the tables and booths full and every seat at the bar taken. She recognized a few people—Ford Hanson was sitting off in the corner with his wife, Morgan. A car seat rested in the brace of a stand at the end of their booth, and Ford was so focused on the baby in it that he didn't even seem to notice that anyone had come in.

But that wasn't the cause of the change in her husband.

Morgan waved, and Roxane waved back.

Again, Roxane looked around the diner but didn't see anything odd. She had only eaten in here a handful of times and never when it was this busy. Some of the other patrons looked familiar, and she didn't recognize either waitress.

One was really pretty in an angelic type of way, slender with blond hair that was pinned into a bun in the back of her head. For as busy as it was, not a hair was out of place. She wore a pink shirt and a below-the-knee khaki skirt, and she walked with a grace and smoothness that Roxane's ballet teacher would salivate at.

But Boone barely glanced at her, and he wasn't the kind of man who would allow his eye to be caught by another woman, anyway.

Whatever it was, the change was so dramatic that when Boone started walking toward an empty booth over against the window that faced the street, Roxane almost resisted following him. Always before, he'd led, but he'd done it in such a way that she felt like he went first to protect her, not because he was The Boss.

But now, for the first time, she felt as if he were dragging her as he walked in front of her.

An odd feeling, because nothing really had changed, other than how she felt. Irritation surged up, and she squelched it, sliding into her seat and watching as Boone slid into his.

He didn't look at her. His shoulders were tense, and he looked out the window like it was an escape route.

Roxane didn't even glance down at her menu on the place mat. "What's wrong?"

HOW COULD SHE TELL there was something wrong?

One minute, he'd been hoping to eat as fast as he could and spend the evening cuddling and maybe making out with his wife, and the next, all he wanted to do was turn around and walk straight back out of the diner.

The new waitress in Sweet Water was Angela Davis. The girl he'd thought he loved and offered to marry this past summer. She'd rejected him.

She was supposed to be married and out of his life. Now she was in his town. Working in the diner.

There were two women in the world that he'd ever had feelings for. He'd been wrong about one. And he was desperate to win the favor of the other.

They were both in the diner tonight.

His past and his future. Hopefully.

He'd walked to the booth quickly, and Angela hadn't seen him yet. He had a bit of time; he might be able to explain what had happened between him and Angela to his wife. He didn't want her to get the wrong idea.

Lots of people had pasts. It's just that he'd not gotten around to telling her about his. And now it was here.

A shadow fell on the table, and he looked up.

His window of opportunity had just closed.

"Boone. I didn't think I would see you until closer to Thanksgiving when the crew is done for the season." Angela put her fingers on his forearm, like they were old friends.

Her nails were blunt with a pale pink polish.

He looked up into her sweet, blue eyes, his stomach churning. He'd been deceived by her appearance for a long time. He hadn't talked to his brother too much about it after the night they'd fought about her, but Clay had been deceived, too.

Angela's family was very concerned about appearances. It reminded Boone of the whited sepulchers that Jesus had spoken of in scriptures.

The outside looked good, and a lot of people were fooled.

He'd been one of them.

It wasn't his proudest moment, and he was going to get to face it with his wife watching.

"Thought you got married." There was no ring on the fingers that gripped his arm. He noticed that, but more disturbing to him was the stiffness of his wife's position. She hadn't moved other than that slight tilt of her head. A sure sign she was putting her nose in the air and wrapping her East Coast high society social status around her like a shield. He hated that she was doing it against him.

"It didn't work out." Angela's jaw tightened. The only sign he could see that there had been something significant going on. He wasn't sure what had kept her from getting married or what had brought her to Sweet Water and working in the diner, but he couldn't even admit to more than a mild curiosity.

He wished she'd leave. He glanced at Roxane. Her face was a mask of social politeness. It didn't surprise him. She'd obviously picked up on the undercurrents.

"I want to talk to you." Angela, too, glanced at Roxane, almost giving the impression that she was conspiring with Boone about needing privacy.

He had no desire to talk to Angela. They had nothing to say to each other.

Roxane slapped her hands down on the table. "Well, you two can talk. I'm going to the ladies' room." She slid to the edge of her seat.

Boone wanted to get out and walk with her. Maybe he'd have a chance to explain what was happening and ease the hard shell that had settled over her face. But Angela's hand was still on his arm. He couldn't get out without pushing into her.

"Wait," he said, not liking the desperation in his voice but not wanting Roxane to leave.

She lifted a brow at him.

"Please," he said, softer.

She didn't say anything but stopped at the edge of her seat, not sliding back, like she was giving him just a few moments.

"We don't have anything to talk about, Angela." He looked at the woman who projected innocence and sweetness. He wouldn't call her family money-grubbers. It was more about projecting the right visuals, maybe even conniving to make other people look bad to make themselves look more spiritual. Or maybe it was more just bulldozing anyone over who got in their way.

He wasn't going to allow that to happen to Roxane, even though he knew she was perfectly capable of standing up for herself.

"I think we do." Angela gave him a slightly superior look before looking down at Roxane. "You don't look like the kind of woman who would allow your date to tell you what to do." She moved, completely blocking Boone. "Go ahead and go. I just need a minute."

"If you have something to say to me, you can say it in front of my wife." Boone didn't even try to make his words come out kindly.

Angela's eyes popped open and flew to his hand. He didn't have a ring, and neither did Roxane. On the ranch, he hadn't been worried about it. Now, he wished he hadn't been so oblivious. A ring was a clear sign to a woman like Angela that he was taken. He wanted the same for Roxane. She was his. And he didn't want there to be any confusion about it. He didn't care if that made him a Neanderthal.

"You're married?" she said, surprise clear in her voice. "But this summer, you professed your undying love for me and begged me to marry you."

Roxane did not make a sound. And she didn't move. But the change in her was instant and real.

And, yeah. Angela knew exactly what she was doing. Her surprise was genuine, but everything else was completely calculated. She'd known exactly what to say to get the reaction she wanted out of Roxane. Boone couldn't believe he'd not seen through her this summer.

He'd had her so high up on a pedestal that he couldn't see what she was really like, apparently.

Across the table, Roxane's eyes held betrayal.

"I didn't profess my undying love." He knew he was quibbling over details, but the look on his wife's face made breathing difficult. Like his ribs were broken.

"You begged me to marry you." She gave him a soft smile.

"You said no, and I walked away. Now I'm married to someone else. If you have anything else to say to me, you can say it in front of my wife." He was being harsh, but he didn't think she'd respond to any other action.

"Some other time." Roxane stood.

Boone slid to the edge of his seat, not sure what he'd do if Angela didn't step back. But she did. At the same time, she took her hand from his arm.

"I thought you were better than that, Boone," she said softly, like he'd hurt her.

Maybe he had. He couldn't really tell. But it seemed like he had a choice between hurting her and hurting his wife. Roxane was his first interest and always would be. He moved to her side, wanting to take her hand but not sure she wouldn't slap him away.

He decided he'd take the chance. And more. He put his arm around her.

She was stiff, but she allowed him to pull her close. Treating him better than he deserved, probably.

She didn't say anything to him but started for the door of the diner. On the way out, they passed Sawyer and Georgia Olson from one of the neighboring ranches. Georgia, her hair as wild as always and seeming even smaller next to her large husband, looked like she had a beach ball under her shirt.

It wasn't something Boone would normally notice, but his eye and thoughts were drawn to the baby she carried because his wife would soon look similar. The thought made him feel good in a way that was hard to explain.

He shook Sawyer's hand and exchanged some comments on the weather and the price of beef and farming in general as his wife chatted with Georgia and set up a time to get together. He was happy about that. He thought she liked it in North Dakota, but it had to be a lot different than she was used to. He didn't want her to be bored and restless. She'd been putting all her energy into the Thanksgiving meal, but once that was over, he wasn't sure what direction she'd want to go. Hopefully not east.

They didn't chat for long, and soon he was opening the door for Roxane to climb into his truck. She didn't look at him, and she didn't say anything.

He closed the door and walked around, knowing this wasn't something that should cause a wedge between them but knowing it could if he didn't handle it right. He should have told her. She shouldn't have found out in a restaurant from the woman he proposed to.

He could joke, and he could take things in stride, but he wasn't great at explaining himself, and he'd never been good with smooth words.

Chapter 16

Roxane stared at the dash, feeling like she was reeling. Boone had asked that woman to marry him *just this summer*. It couldn't have been long before Clay's wedding. Which, of course, made her wonder if what had happened at Clay's wedding had anything to do with his broken heart and a rebound relationship or whatever one wanted to call it.

Angela had been fair and pretty and perfect and everything Roxane would have thought Boone would want in a woman.

Still, he didn't seem heartbroken, and he didn't seem tempted, but her rational thoughts hadn't been able to get her emotional chaos under control. It didn't take much to upset her stomach nowadays, and it felt like she'd swallowed a bottle of glue, cramping and sticky.

Boone started the truck and pulled out without saying anything, pointing it in the direction of home and driving like he always did, methodically, with no outward sign of anger or distress. If he were upset that he'd not gotten food or that she'd aborted their date, he didn't show it.

He wasn't joking, either, though. And that was unusual.

Sweet Water Ranch wasn't far, but before they got there, he turned off onto a dirt road that led between two fields with different lengths of a cover crop growing. She thought the fields belonged to Sweet Water Ranch, but honestly, she wasn't sure.

He drove slowly down the dirt path for what felt like a long time. She had no clue where they were, but she trusted Boone with all her heart.

Which is one of the reasons she knew, even if he did still have feelings for the blond, he would never act on them. But there was something in her heart that rebelled at having her husband stay true because he had to rather than wanted to. Maybe it was her feminine vanity that was offended.

Either way, she recognized her childishness but hadn't quite gotten a handle on it by the time he stopped.

His hands stayed together on top of the steering wheel, and he kept his face forward. His chest went in and out twice before he spoke.

"I'm sorry about that."

She swallowed and looked away, not sure she was ready to have a mature conversation about it yet.

"I have a blanket in my blizzard kit behind the seat. I was hoping I could lay it out on the ground, and you'd sit with me for a bit." He blew a long breath out his nose and finally looked over at her.

She pulled her lips in, knowing he hadn't done anything wrong, feeling bad because he obviously felt like he did, but unable to force the words out of her mouth that would ease his burden. Whatever happened in his past wasn't up for her to judge...except, everyone—herself and Boone included—would be fools to dismiss the past because the future was predicated upon it.

Still, there were a lot of things in her past that Boone had overlooked, whether they indicated a deficiency in her character or not.

"I will," she said, opening her door before he told her to wait, that he would get it. She appreciated the consideration, and loved what it said about his values and character, but just wasn't ready to give in.

He spread the blanket out on her side of the truck, ten feet or so into the field. "This rye is high enough that it will make an almost comfortable cushion."

She bent, helping to pull out a corner before stepping on the edge. She sat down, dividing the blanket up into two imaginary sides and sitting well to the edge of hers.

"I actually had two blankets." He held another up, shaking it out and arranging it around her shoulders.

"Thanks."

He wasn't being considerate to butter her up. This was the way he always was.

He sprawled out beside her, on his back, tucking both hands under his head and staring up. "The most beautiful night sky that I've ever seen is here in North Dakota."

She couldn't disagree. "I guess you'd know."

There was no moon, but she could see his throat work. "I told you where I've been. I haven't deliberately hidden anything."

"You just neglected to mention Angela."

"You never talk about Bryan."

"That's because he's a jerk."

"That you were married to. That you have a child with. You made vows with him—"

"He broke them! Not just once but over and over. There's nothing to say, other than I wouldn't be upset to never see him again."

He pushed up on his elbows and turned toward her. "I know all that. And I believe it. But there's a lot of stuff I don't know. If he came tomorrow, you and he could talk for hours about things I've never heard of. And you can't tell me there weren't good times." He seemed to search her face in the darkness. She studied his eyes before turning and looking up at the brightness of the stars.

"You're right. There were."

He didn't push his advantage, making her feel like it wasn't a fight. "I'm sorry I didn't mention Angela. My brother wrote to her for years. Her parents wouldn't let him do any more than just look at her from a safe distance. You don't know Clay well, but that's all he needed. He'd set his mind, and he was willing to wait, to follow the rules. I admired Angela, but because I love Clay, I would never have said anything." He turned his face back to the stars. "She looks good from a distance."

A smile hovered around Roxane's mouth. He didn't have to mention Angela and her similarity to the stars. Looked good from a distance, but she wouldn't want to touch one. She laughed a little, and when he turned his head, he was smiling too. They grinned at their shared joke.

She moved the blanket from her shoulders and lay back on her elbows, imitating his position but not touching him.

The tension had eased between them—funny how laughing together did that—but he still hadn't gotten to the part she wanted to hear.

She didn't have the patience to wait. "And?"

"Then Reina entered the picture, and I guess Clay realized which one was real and which one wasn't." He shook his head a little. "Please don't misunderstand. I know you can look like Angela does and be good on the inside too. She's just not."

"Where do you come in?" She felt like if she just waited, he'd tell her. Waiting had never been something she was good at.

His shoulders moved like it was obvious. "I was still blinded. I thought Clay was not treating her well." He moved again, rolling to his side, facing her with his head propped in his hand. Not speaking for a moment, as though gathering his thoughts, he finally opened his mouth. "Clay and I actually fought over it. I fought. Clay understood what I was going through because he'd done the same thing. I wouldn't tell this to just anyone, but Angela's family needed money, and Clay could have given it to her. I was angry that he was choosing Reina instead. When I spoke with Angela after Clay and I had words, that's when I asked...begged her to choose me." He closed his mouth, and his lip twisted back, as though he was frustrated with himself.

"She laughed a little, like the idea of her and I was something she would never consider." He lifted a shoulder. "She said some things that made me realize that it was all about looks." He snorted. "And at that point, money talked, too. And I didn't have what it took."

He rolled back over and put his hands behind his head, looking at the stars, although she doubted he was seeing them.

"I'm not carrying a torch for her. I don't know what she wanted tonight. I don't care. Not even curious." He turned his head without moving the rest of his body. "And that's the truth."

She believed it. Except...

"Is that how you felt at Clay's wedding?" Her voice sounded as thready as the lone cricket that had somehow lived through the frost and freezes of the cool fall nights and chirped not far from where they lay.

His head turned. His brows furrowed, like he was trying to figure out where in the world she was going with that question. His mouth was opened a little, and she could almost see his brain working, going back through the things that had happened, and trying to figure out what Angela had to do with any of it.

Her fears that he'd been thinking of Angela that day eased.

He rolled again, this time coming within a few inches of her as he lay on his side with his head propped in his hand. He used one finger to touch the track of the tear that she'd not even realized had come out of her eye.

"I don't understand. Help me." His hand cupped her cheek then smoothed along her jawline like he couldn't stop touching her. He dragged it away, resting it on the blanket between them.

"I thought you might have been still thinking of her. I thought maybe that's why you allowed me to persuade you to..." She turned her head away.

His hand came back, landing softly on her cheek. "No." His lips touched her forehead. "No." They brushed against her skin, his whispered word floating between them.

She closed her eyes, knowing he was speaking the truth.

His lips moved again, and she shivered.

"You're cold?" he asked softly.

"Yes." It wasn't quite the truth, but he reacted the way she'd known he would, sliding closer and putting his arm around her. She rested her head on his bicep.

"Better?"

"Yes." Everything was better. Maybe she was more emotional because of the baby. She didn't usually need to be reassured. Or maybe she just cared more.

More than likely, she was falling in love with her husband, and she was worried that he might not feel the same. He was honest and open, and if he loved her, she was pretty sure he wouldn't sit around wondering whether or not he should tell her.

She turned toward him and put her arm around him, throwing one leg over his, snuggling deeper, not even pretending to be looking at the stars. But a lifetime with the man holding her was starting to look more beautiful than all the stars the heavens could hold.

IT WAS STILL DARK WHEN Boone came in from the barn the next morning. He hadn't been able to sleep, so he'd gotten up earlier than usual and done the feeding. The cows and horses didn't mind, and they were out in the barn right now, happily eating.

But he'd been restless.

There was plenty of work to do but not too much that could be done before daylight.

He knew Roxane wouldn't be up.

Mrs. Sprouse wouldn't be up, either.

He didn't know why he was going to the house.

Yeah, he did. Because Roxane was there, and he wanted to be where she was.

He walked through the office and into the kitchen, unsure what, exactly, he was going to do, other than pace in there like he'd been doing in the barn.

As he strode past the bar, a white envelope caught his eye.

It was addressed to both of them and came from a law office. They must have missed it last night in their hurry to go out.

He picked it up and walked over to the sink, holding it under the light that stayed on all night.

Unopened.

He didn't hesitate but tore the envelope. Maybe this was their test. He'd wondered what it was, and it was about the time the lawyer had said.

His eyes skimmed down over the words on the page. It was, indeed, their test.

His first instinct was to hide the letter. He didn't want Roxane to see it. His heart shivered in a way it never had before, and the paper rustled softly in hands that had started to tremble.

For him, this was easy. He didn't have to think, not for even a second.

But for Roxane...he didn't know. He suspected she might have a harder time making up her mind.

He flattened the letter out and laid it on the counter. She'd see it when she came downstairs this morning. He slipped back outside, determined to find something to do that would keep him from thinking about the decision his wife had two weeks to make.

BOONE MET HIS MOTHER coming out of the office when he finally stopped for lunch, forty-five minutes late.

She gave him a look that only mothers do, sweeping over him from head to toe and taking in everything. "You've lost weight." She chuckled a little. "Most of the time when men get married, they gain weight."

Well, he hadn't eaten since yesterday lunch, but that was hardly going to make him lose enough that his mother would notice. "I think you're imagining things, Mom."

"You're a little late for lunch. Looks like you were really into something." She eyed his dirty clothes and hands. Probably his face was just as bad.

"Digging up the septic system on one of the cabins out back."

"That's been leaking for years, but no one's ever in it."

"Needs to be done."

"I see." Her pressed lips said she probably did see. He wasn't sure he wanted her to. She pulled her purse farther up her shoulder. "I'm going out to see Lark and won't be back. I think Roxane's waiting on you. Mrs. Sprouse left supper, but her husband had an appointment in Rockerton, so she won't be around, either."

"I think we'll manage."

Her mother put a hand on his arm. "Maybe you ought to take it a little easy on your wife. She looks exhausted."

He blinked at his mother, trying to figure out if she was really saying what he thought she was saying.

"Let her sleep, honey."

Yep. He was pretty sure she was. He supposed he should be happy about that, because obviously, she didn't realize he was sleeping in the barn. He shook his head, mostly at the weirdness of life sometimes, and said, "Yeah, Mom. I'll do that."

"I'll see you tomorrow." She gave him one last, hard look then moved down the path to her car.

Normally he couldn't wait to see his wife, whether he'd been gone for five minutes or five hours, but today his feet dragged.

She was sitting at the bar with the folder that she used to keep all the things she was organizing for the Thanksgiving meal that was coming up soon.

He stopped in the doorway.

She was beautiful, as always, even with the dark circles around her eyes. Her hair flowed over her shoulder, and her dark orange shirt brought out the amber of her eyes, which were wide and staring at him.

Sometimes, he wondered what she saw when she looked at him. Someone a lot different than the first man she'd chosen to marry. He didn't have an Ivy League education and blue-blood pedigree. He never figured that mattered. It sure didn't to him, but those things were important to some people.

Her eyes softened, and he almost thought he saw a smile tilt one corner of her mouth. Maybe she was remembering last night, too. He'd never kissed her like he'd said he was going to do, but they'd snuggled under the stars for a long time, and it had been better than kissing in some ways.

"Hey." She didn't move.

Tempted to tell her what his mom had just said, because it would make her smile, he caught sight of the letter that lay between them, and he clamped his mouth shut.

"Feeling okay?" he asked instead.

She nodded.

He was going to eat before he dealt with it. Or at least while he dealt with it. He washed his hands then went to the fridge and pulled out leftover chicken from the day before. "You want a sandwich?"

"No thanks."

He wanted to give her a hard time about eating for the baby but decided today wasn't the day. "You saw the letter."

"Yes," she said, even though he hadn't really meant it as a question.

He paused, a piece of chicken in his hand. She was looking at him like she wasn't sure what he thought.

Rather than bothering with a sandwich, he put a piece of chicken in his mouth, chewed, and swallowed. "It said our test was that if we wanted to keep the ranch, we had to call it quits."

"Divorce." She said the word he didn't want to say. "And one of us has to leave."

That's what he'd read too. "The other one gets a billion dollars."

"If we decide to stay together, we have to move off the ranch."

"And we get no money."

She nodded. Yeah, that's what he'd thought. He chewed on some more chicken.

"I don't need two weeks to think about this, Roxane."

"I don't, either."

That surprised him. But he looked at the determination in her eye. There was something else there too. Something that gave him hope. His mouth kicked up. "We're moving?"

She smiled. "Yes."

Chapter 17

Boone couldn't hide the shock that ripped through his chest. "This is your family's ranch."

"It can become someone else's ranch."

A pang hit his chest. He'd been about to eat another piece of chicken, but he slowly lowered his hand. "Were you thinking we'd go east?"

She lifted her brows. "Would you?"

Before he could answer, her phone rang. It sounded like it might be one of her friends from New York. He listened with half an ear while he chewed, grabbing a drink of water from the sink.

Surely she didn't really want to move to New York. Although he could probably handle that, as long as it was a portion of New York that had farms and fields and plenty of room for a man to spread out, even if he didn't care for some of their stifling laws. Maybe because he traveled around through so many states while harvesting, but he was hyper-aware that state laws could be vastly different.

But he'd go.

Even if she wanted to live in the city where she came from, if she refused to live with him anywhere else, he thought he could do it. Maybe.

He almost snorted. He would. He didn't want to, but he would. If that's what she wanted. After all, if she could place herself on an auction block and let a stranger buy her, he could live in the city. He'd try, anyway. For Roxane.

He was done eating by the time she got off the phone and was just putting the empty bowl in the dishwasher.

"We're getting company." She stood up from her stool.

He looked up. "Now?"

She took a breath, looking around. "In about four hours. My mom and two of my friends, using the word loosely, since neither of them wanted to have too much to do with me when Bryan and I split." She drummed her fingers on the countertop. "I can get the bedrooms ready, and I can figure something out to eat. They're leaving Sunday afternoon, so it won't be a huge deal, but..." Her voice trailed off, and she bit her lip.

He held his hands out. "I'm filthy, but I can change. I'm not doing anything that can't wait until next week to finish. What do you need?"

She lifted her chin in that familiar way she had, and he knew whatever she was going to ask would be something extremely hard. He'd kill himself to do it for her.

"I need you to sleep with me."

His empty glass slipped out of his hand. Thankfully it was only an inch off the counter and didn't break, although it made a loud crash that echoed in the quiet kitchen.

"That didn't come out right." Roxane's eyes watched his glass like she could keep him from dropping it again by staring at it. "I know you're staying in the barn because we got things a little backward and other things should have happened first and that wasn't what you'd wanted and you were trying to do everything right or make up for it in some way or whatever that was—"

"Stop, please." He held his hand up. He'd never heard Roxane ramble like that. He kind of liked it, since she was always so cool and collected and made him feel like rambling.

She clamped her mouth shut like she knew she was throwing up words.

He narrowed his eyes and moved around the end of the bar. One of her eyes closed a little like she was lining up a bead. He didn't let that stop him, because he was pretty sure that wasn't what she was doing.

"I was out in the barn," he stepped closer, "because I wanted you to know—"

She took a step back.

"—that you meant more to me—"

Her hip hit the far countertop, and she stopped.

"—than what it looked like at Clay's wedding." He stopped in front of her, wanting to put his arms around her but needing to talk to her first.

Her head tilted up. "You're not scaring me."

He snorted a laugh. "Your backing up was strategic?"

"It wasn't fear."

"Good. I'd be real upset if you were scared of me."

"So you were stalking me, but not to scare me?"

"I haven't seen you scared yet. Not on the auction block and not in the kitchen. I hardly think I'd cause that emotion in you."

She opened her mouth, but he put one finger over it. "You've changed the subject."

She bit his finger.

It hurt. Really. But he laughed. "I think you're avoiding this conversation, which makes me really curious as to why?"

She opened her mouth, and he pulled his finger out, allowing himself to wrap his hand around her neck and push his fingers into the soft hair at the nape of her neck.

"Maybe I have other thoughts about that."

"About what?"

"About what happened at the wedding."

That's right. He knew how she felt. He'd been awkward and clumsy and who knew what else. He looked away, all the teasing draining out of him. Regret taking its place.

She touched him, her hand on his cheek, and he froze. "Maybe I see it differently than you do."

His cheek ached to lean into her hand, pressing closer, but he stayed still, shifting only his eyes to hers, waiting.

"I'm not disagreeing that it wasn't the right way to start a relation-ship, but I knew from that time what kind of man you were. A good man. One who probably had the opportunity but had never disap-peared into dark rooms with anyone before. Who didn't treat women as disposable. Who wasn't out for himself and what he could get with-out a care about the emotional destruction he left behind. Someone who valued me and made me feel more cherished than I ever had in my life before." She took a shallow breath. "Someone as different from my ex-husband as he could be." Her hand moved on his cheek. "It doesn't make sense, and I don't regret it, not a second of it, but I've wished every day since that I hadn't pushed you into shedding your morals and everything you valued and going with me."

"No," he said immediately. "You can't blame yourself for my lack."

"It was my lack, too."

"You didn't choose for me. I chose. Like David looking at Bathshe-ba. Maybe I shouldn't have been dancing with you to begin with."

"I'm glad you were."

He put his hand over hers. "It's too late to have regrets. Plus, I can see how everything tied together, and the Lord worked it out." He just couldn't help but feel like God wasn't done. He couldn't settle in and be comfortable.

"I know my timing is bad because my mother and friends are com-ing, but I really would like to see you move out of the barn and into the house. Where you belong." She moved then, and her other hand came up, resting on his waist.

"You're saying you want me in your room because of me and not because of how it will look to your mom," he asked, unable to keep from teasing her.

"I could move out to the barn. That would really shock everyone."

"Me included." He put his arms around her and drew her close. "Your bed sounds nicer, but I'll sleep in the barn with you too. Your choice." It wasn't like it was going to matter in two weeks, anyway.

"Once we tell the lawyer we're choosing to stay together, I wonder how long we'll have to move out. Maybe we should start packing."

"I'm not packing before the Thanksgiving meal. There aren't going to be boxes and junk scattered everywhere."

"I only have my clothes and my truck. I don't need boxes."

"Regardless, I will not allow them to just throw us out. There will be a set time, and it will be reasonable." She looked up at him, her face set.

He had to grin. He loved that take-charge attitude. "I was going to recommend that you take my mom's place and control the finances of the ranch, since you have experience in business anyway, but I guess it's not something we need to think about anymore."

She tilted her head. "You don't think your mom would mind?"

"She's said for years that she'd like to be able to stay on the ranch. Now that it's paid for, and with all the boys to help her with the field-work, she could putter around the house and barn to her heart's content."

"That's too bad. Maybe when Sweet Water sells, she'll quit."

"Maybe." He ran his hands down her back. "What do we have to do before your mom and friends get here?"

"Not much." She shrugged.

"Then I have time to kiss you."

Her hand tightened on his hip. The one still on his cheek moved around to the back of his head and pulled. She hadn't said anything, but she didn't need to.

He might be thick and even dumb when it came to women, but there was no question what the tugging on the back of his head meant.

WHEN THE DOORBELL RANG a few hours later, they hadn't gotten much cleaning done at all. Boone couldn't quit smiling, and she was in a fabulous mood herself. Way too good of a mood to have to deal with her mother.

But she did, and despite the fact that she could tell her mother and her two friends didn't think Boone's jeans and boots and soft flannel shirt were quite up to their standards, Boone was his normal easygoing self. Their visit went well. She kind of thought it might drag, but before she knew it, it was Sunday afternoon and they were standing on the porch waving goodbye.

"I would have gone and picked up Spencer so he could see his gram." Boone had his arm around Roxane's shoulders, and he squeezed her to him when he spoke.

"I texted him, but he didn't care to see her. Maybe you didn't notice, but she didn't even ask about him. She doesn't really care for little boys. They're too loud and messy." Roxane could hear the bitterness, or maybe it was sadness, in her tone. She forced a better outlook. "She might feel differently about a little girl."

Boone grinned, turning to her and putting a hand on her stomach. "You're so sure it's a girl. How?"

She put her hand over the top of his and pressed gently. "I just know."

He lowered his head to kiss her, and she thought her world could not be more perfect.

Except before his lips touched hers, a sharp pain ripped through her stomach.

She'd barely flinched before Boone asked, "What's wrong?"

Both of her hands were wrapped around her stomach, and she was doubled over. "I don't know," she grunted out. "It hurts."

Fear spiked through her, worse than the pain. It grabbed her lungs and seized her heart and scraped its icy claws down her backbone.

She recognized the pain. She'd felt something very similar when Spencer was born. Only it had felt natural then. A little scary, but not the gripping fear that had her heart in a vice right now.

"Will you be okay here while I go get my truck and bring it right here? I'm taking you to the ER." He was backing away as he said it, getting ready to run, she assumed.

"No," she said, her head bent and staring at the floor.

He stopped abruptly. Then he pulled his phone out of his pocket. "I'm calling 911."

"No," she ground out again.

"Holy frig, woman. You can't think I'm just going to stand here and watch this."

"Then go somewhere else."

"Isn't there a chance we can do something? Something to stop it?"

He'd figured out what was happening. She supposed she ought to feel grateful she didn't have to explain it to him. But she didn't. She hurt, sharp, burning pain that pushed like a bulldozer through her stomach and ripped backward and cramped down her legs and through her chest.

"No." She swallowed hard. "I'm only nine weeks. They can't do anything." She'd volunteered at a woman's shelter one summer before college. More because it would look good on her college application than because she was a saint. She'd seen one of the girls there go through a miscarriage.

It seemed to feel very much like childbirth. Like the pain felt so bad she thought it was going to kill her, and then it got worse and worse until she wished it would.

He still had his phone out; maybe he was searching the internet for what to do.

She put her hand on his knee because she couldn't straighten to put it on his chest. "Would you carry me inside, please?"

MONDAY NIGHT, ROXANE finally slept. The pain seemed to be mostly gone, and she'd huddled under the blankets in their bed. Boone had slid in beside her, but when he touched her, she'd stiffened, so he'd rolled over on his back and waited until her breathing was deep and steady. He slid out and slipped on a pair of jeans, walking downstairs in his bare feet and outside into the cold North Dakota night, sitting down on the step, and easing the ache in his back by setting both elbows on his knees.

He hadn't done anything in his life that had been harder than the last two days. Not that Roxane had been unkind or complained. But it was harder than he'd ever imagined to see the suffering of someone he loved so fiercely. Not to mention, he'd been scared beyond words that she was going to die. And she wouldn't let him call to take her anywhere.

It seemed like she was going to be okay. Physically.

He'd read enough on the internet, though, to recognize immediately that the emotional scarring could be worse than the physical pain. If that were true, he had no idea what to do. He couldn't really imagine anything worse than the pain and the blood, but the crying that she had done this evening had ripped him raw.

It hurt almost as badly that she didn't want him to touch her.

Any time before when he'd been hurt emotionally—he wouldn't even have admitted that he was hurt—he'd just go and work it out. Something hard. Like digging up a septic tank. Changing tires on a tractor. Painting the barn, with a toothbrush. Okay, so he hadn't ever actually done that last one, but he'd been tempted to hand one to Spencer when he'd gotten home from school. Thankfully the boy had been outside with Bill until dark and had been satisfied with Boone's answer of "she's sick" when he'd asked where his mother was.

But Boone couldn't go outside and work while Roxane was inside, crying.

The cold air felt good. Sharp and hard on his feet, especially, but good in the way it gave him something to fight against. Something to win against.

He didn't have a problem thinking about the child they'd lost. A daughter, if Roxie were right, as she was so sure she was.

It was easy to picture her in heaven, laughing and running around with the other children. According to the numbers he'd seen while looking it up, because how could he not, three thousand children per day joined her.

He wasn't a heaven scholar, but he did think that time was maybe different there. But he had no doubt where his child was. It was almost a blessing to think of her safe in the arms of Jesus. He'd be a better father than Boone, anyway.

But being a good husband was what concerned him now. He felt like he was failing.

Maybe Roxane blamed him for the miscarriage. The last words she'd spoken to him had been asking him to carry her in. Other than yes or no when he offered her water and food.

He could only pray that tomorrow was different.

Chapter 18

By Tuesday, Roxane was out of bed. The pain had stopped at least. Physical pain.

Rationally, she knew the hormones were messing with her head, so she felt she was better off not saying anything than saying a bunch of stuff she'd regret.

Like the miscarriage was Boone's fault. It wasn't true. She knew it. But she still wanted to say it. To blame him. To have a place to vent her anger.

Thing was, she knew he'd take it. She could scream at him and say as many hurtful things as she wanted, and her husband would stand and take it. As sure as she knew her name, she knew that to be an indisputable fact.

Maybe that was why she couldn't do it.

With a lot of effort, she was able to act almost normally for the few hours per day that she saw Spencer.

Otherwise, she avoided Boone. He went to bed with her. But she couldn't stand for him to touch her. Not for comfort, not for warmth, not for anything. She wasn't sure why. Hormones making her crazy probably.

Rationally, again, she could see it was wrong, but she couldn't keep from feeling like she couldn't stand to be touched.

How did one come to terms with the death of their child? How could she just keep on living like nothing had happened? Like the life had never been there?

The pregnancy calendar she'd had on her phone mocked her every morning with a notification and a short fact about her baby's development.

The bib that she'd picked up on an impulse buy at the feed store the last time Boone and she had gone in for supplies lay faceup on her dresser. It had a picture of a green tractor and said, "My daddy drives a Deere." It had hit all of her pregnancy-hormone-induced buttons, and she smiled every time she looked at it.

Not anymore.

There were the messages on social media asking how she was feeling and how her morning sickness was going and the worst, a text from her friend who'd just been here that said she had a gorgeous husband and their baby was sure to be beautiful.

She'd stopped carrying her phone around.

The entire thing was just too painful.

But the Monday a week after her miscarriage, her physical symptoms were all but gone and she had to pull herself together. There was a Thanksgiving feast happening at Sweet Water on Saturday, and she was responsible for making it happen. So she put her chin up, dug in, and got to work hanging and arranging the decorations that Boone had helped her make over the last month or so.

"NEED ME TO HELP?"

Roxane couldn't believe Boone was still offering. She'd declined his help every time he offered, three or four times a day, every day since she started working on Monday. It was Friday lunch time, and he was still offering.

"No thank you," she said tightly, not looking at him. She didn't understand why he wouldn't just leave her alone. She didn't want to feel anything for anyone. Feeling things for people meant pain, and she'd had enough of that to last her a lifetime.

Boone was a nice man, but she didn't want to see him, didn't want to talk to him, didn't want to work with him, and definitely didn't want him touching her. She might break.

"Talk to me, Roxie, please?"

They were in the big ballroom. The same room where her brother had chosen the love of his life.

She hadn't even told her family she'd lost the baby.

The entire town knew about her pregnancy, thanks to Boone's big mouth at the auction, but no one knew about the miscarriage.

Unless Boone had told people.

She adjusted a burnt orange ribbon on the cornucopia she and Boone had made before her child had died. "Did you tell anyone?"

"Do you hate me so much you can't look at me when you're talking to me?" he returned.

"I don't hate you." Her answer was rote and automatic, but still true. The emotions she felt for him were strong, and they weren't hate. Maybe she hated what she felt. Hated feeling anything.

"Then why are you punishing me?"

"I'm not punishing you. I'm working through the stages of grief." That was a total crock. She might have known what the stages were at one time, but she wasn't working through anything. She was protecting herself.

"Couldn't we work through our grief together?" he asked, and there was no mistaking the pleading in his tone.

She didn't deserve his kindness nor his patience. Maybe she'd feel better if he actually got angry at her. Probably not. It would only give her ammunition to use against him.

"What grief? You don't seem to have any," she snapped at him, moving to the windowsill and the fall-colored leaves that were arranged there. Her accusation was unfair. Just because he wasn't acting like her didn't mean he wasn't grieving. She'd seen his face when they heard the heartbeat. His hand had been held protectively over their child when the first pain started. She knew he grieved.

He put his hand on the windowsill, directly in her line of vision. Her hands stopped, but she didn't look at him.

He slapped the windowsill. The crack reverberated in the huge ballroom. Roxane flinched.

"I lost my child *and* my wife. How can I not be grieving?"

She pointed at his face. "Your eyes are dry. I've seen you smile. And you walk around like you don't have a care in the world. If you're grieving, I'm a moon rock."

It wasn't fair. She knew it wasn't fair. He didn't have to show his grief like she did. She didn't expect him to. He wasn't dealing with her hormones, either, or the body that still wasn't fully healed. But she couldn't keep from striking at him.

He didn't break down in sobs. His eyes didn't even water. He stared at her in stony silence.

His jaw jutted out. "I see my child running on the golden streets of heaven. I see her playing with other children and asking Jesus if it's time yet. I don't want to die, but when I do, I'm gonna walk through those gates and she's gonna come running. She's gonna wrap her arms around my legs and squeeze tight, and she's gonna say, 'Welcome home, Daddy.' She's gonna have your amazing eyes and that stubborn chin and that aristocratic nose that you put in the air every time you have something hard to do, and maybe she'll have my smile and maybe a dimple, and I'm gonna pick her up and hug her for the first time ever. I'm gonna admire the child that we made together and hold her and get to know her. And all the pain of now will be worthwhile when I see her innocence and joy, and I'll see clearly then what I only guess at now, and I'll know that there was no better place for her to grow up, no more love or care or protection that she could have had, even if it meant that I had to wait a little longer to meet her than I wanted."

He slapped his hand on the sill, not as hard this time, before he turned. "I'm going to haul hay bales."

His boots clicked on the floor as he walked out.

Tempted to turn and watch him go, even more tempted to run after him, Roxane turned to her left. Mrs. Stryker was standing in the doorway that led to the courtyard.

"I'm sorry, honey," she said, walking slowly in. "I heard a big crack and came in to see if you were okay."

"I'm fine," Roxane said automatically.

Mrs. Stryker kept walking, and she didn't stop until she had her arms wrapped around Roxane. "I'm sorry, sweetie. I didn't know."

Roxane couldn't do anything but hug her back, clinging to the older woman, the mother of her husband.

"When?" Mrs. Stryker asked, her arms squeezing and feeling good and solid.

"Last Sunday night."

"Oh, my poor, brave girl. You've been hurting all week and working anyway." She patted her back.

Roxane had known she wouldn't be able to take the comfort. Not without completely falling apart. She sobbed in Mrs. Stryker's arms for a long time.

Mrs. Stryker didn't say anything more, and Roxane didn't need her to.

When the door opened and Spencer's voice called out, she couldn't believe the time that had flown by.

"I need to talk to him." She pulled away from her mother-in-law.

Mrs. Stryker nodded. Roxane expected her to prompt her to go to her husband and talk to him, too, but she didn't need the reminder and Mrs. Stryker didn't give it.

Roxane hurried to the kitchen where Spencer was digging in the fridge. "Hey, honey. I'm glad you're home."

He turned, a carrot stick in his mouth. His brow puckered. "Were you crying?" He slowly chewed while fear started to cross his face.

"I was." She walked forward and put a hand on his shoulder. "The baby that I was carrying went to heaven and will grow up there."

His nose wrinkled. "Why?"

She could only answer honestly. "I don't know."

"Why are you crying? Heaven's good, right?" He put the rest of the carrot in his mouth.

"You're right. It's good." She wiped the last of the tears from her cheeks. "It just seems like it's far away sometimes."

He nodded, chewing, eyeing the pies and other desserts that lined the counter. The refrigerator was bursting with prepared food as well, and Mrs. Sprouse and the two women Roxane had hired would be up before dawn and in the kitchen, cooking.

Roxane knew what her limitations were, and her talents were best suited for decorating and setting up the tables in the ballroom.

But everything that needed to be prepared was ready.

And she had some apologizing to do to her husband.

"Mr. Bill said I could help him clean the barn in case any of the guests wander out there tomorrow."

"That's fine. Change your clothes first." Roxane took one last look around the bustling kitchen, waved at Mrs. Sprouse, and walked out. She needed to find Boone.

It wasn't hard.

He was standing in front of a red car talking to the blond waitress.

There was a part of Roxane that still felt fragile. Like she needed to hide and heal.

But there was another, bigger part that knew the waitress to be a threat. So she didn't retreat to lick her wounds that still felt raw but rather strode out of the door and down the path to the car.

Maybe she looked a little militant, because Boone's eyes widened when he saw her coming. But a corner of his mouth tugged up, and she got the impression he liked the bossy, take-charge aspect of her personality. At least a little. It was the part she tried the hardest to control, and she appreciated the fact that it didn't seem off-putting to her husband. On the contrary, he seemed to admire it.

He also did not seem to be holding a grudge about her recent behavior.

She, on the other hand, didn't like how close the waitress was standing, and even though Boone had told her their history, there was a part of her that had been betrayed by Bryan too many times to fully trust.

The smile on her face was obviously fake, but Roxane stopped beside her husband and turned it on the waitress, whose mouth turned down.

What was her name? "Hello, Angela." She thought that was right.

"Hello. I was stealing your husband for a bit." A gentle smile eased across her face. "I hope that's okay."

"Actually, no. We've got a lot going on here, and I needed to talk to him."

Boone's mouth twitched, but he didn't smile. He did, however, put his arm around her. She relaxed against his side. It felt right to be there. There was still pain in her heart, but her thinking had cleared.

"I can't help you anyway, Angela. I'd have to drive it to hear what tapping sound you're talking about, and you'd be just as well off going to Boyd's Garage that just opened on the other end of Sweet Water."

Angela's lip came out, and her clear blue eyes filled with water. "I can't afford it," she whispered.

A gust of wind blew a whirl of dust across the yard. Spencer came bursting out of the house and went flying by them, yelling that he was going to help Bill.

The silence between them stretched.

Roxane waited for Boone to say that he'd look at her car. But he kept his arm around her and didn't offer anything.

She had to assume that it was up to her to make the decision to either send her on her way or offer to try to fix it.

Even as a woman, she couldn't tell if the tears were real. But it didn't matter. She couldn't see another person who needed help and not offer to do everything she could to fix the problem. Even if it were a woman her husband had history with.

"You take it to Boyd. I'll call him as soon as you leave and give him my card number, authorizing payment on any repairs he makes to your car. In return, I ask that you not touch my husband." She gazed pointedly at Angela's fingers which were wrapped around Boone's forearm.

"You two say you're married. I don't see rings."

"It's my fault," Boone said immediately. He shifted, and Angela's hand finally dropped from his arm. "We have a big day tomorrow, but after that, my schedule is clear." His arm slid down Roxane's back, and his gaze roved over her face. "Maybe you'd come with me to pick out rings?"

"Hey, Boone! I've got a water leak in the barn here, and I need your help." Bill came out of the barn, running. "I'm grabbing some tools and shutting the valve off." He disappeared inside the shed.

"I'd better take care of this." Boone's voice held concern, but his eyes seemed to wait for Roxane's nod.

"It's fine. We'll talk later."

He kissed her forehead then turned and ran after Bill.

Roxane hadn't gotten to apologize, and she was tempted to yell after him as he jogged away. But she didn't. She turned to Angela.

"I thought you just got married. Where's your husband?"

Angela's jaw hardened, but her eyes skidded to the side. "I caught him with one of the stagehand's wives. We'd been married ten days." Her slender shoulders came up and so did her chin. "My parents would take me back, but a divorce would be an embarrassment for them."

"Do you have family here?"

Angela's lip trembled just slightly before she smoothed her features. "No. I just knew Clay was here, and his crew members, and they'd always treated me well."

Roxane felt like Angela had some growing to do, but didn't everyone? She didn't want to be besties, not yet, but she gave her a little smile. "Is there really a tapping in your car?"

Angela's lip pulled back. "Yes. I didn't make it up."

"Take it to Boyd. He'll be fair. And I'll make sure it gets paid for."

Angela was quiet for a moment. "Thanks," she finally said.

"There are signs up all over town, but we're having a Thanksgiving meal here tomorrow, and you're welcome to come." She almost added, *only if you can keep your hands off my husband*, but she figured that would be catty, and she didn't want to be mean.

"Thanks. The diner's closing for it. I'll be here." A little smile crossed her face before she turned and got in her car.

Roxane was tempted to walk to the barn and see what Boone was doing. She realized she'd missed their time together, and she felt especially bad since she could see how much Boone had been hurting too. And she'd shut him out. That had been foolish on her part. Even if he weren't hurting, she was his wife, and she couldn't indulge in catering to herself and excluding him. Not if she wanted her marriage to be strong.

She could have a rock-solid marriage with Boone. It was really up to her. If she could get past her fear and be willing to trust. Maybe that was part of the reason she'd been shutting him out. It hurt too much to share the pain. But her selfishness had been hurting him.

She walked past the kitchen and into the ballroom, running a hand over a perfectly set and decorated table. The decorations were done, the places set, the tables arranged at one end so people could dance at the other end. The speakers were built in, and she had the music chosen. Everything would be perfect...if she was able to fix things between herself and her husband.

She could try.

Chapter 19

B oone walked in, bone weary and wet.

His spirit was good, though. He thought that Roxane might be finally coming around. He hoped so. He'd been lonely without her, hadn't realized how much he'd come to enjoy having her around. Smiling with her. Working. Laughing. Everything was better with his wife beside him.

It could simply have been having company while he worked, but he knew that wasn't quite it. After all, he'd spent years working with his brothers and best friends, and he'd never looked forward to seeing them like he did Roxane.

But it was Angela's visit today that had shown him for real what was going on.

He'd been dismayed to see her. Annoyed that he had to spend time with her and eager to get away from her. If he'd ended up married to her—and he was relieved beyond words that he'd escaped such a fate—he would have figured something out. But it had made him think.

Not long. It hadn't taken much thinking to realize he was in love with his wife.

He wanted to tell her.

Maybe she didn't return his feelings, but that was a chance he'd take. She needed to know where he stood.

He walked on his stocking feet through the dark and quiet kitchen. Tomorrow, no, later today, since it was almost one a.m., it would be bustling, but tonight, it was still, although it smelled amazing.

He'd sent Spencer to bed around eleven. He supposed it was too much to hope for that Roxane was still up. They probably wouldn't have time to talk in the morning. Things would be busy and crazy.

He had his foot on the bottom step when he realized there was music playing, soft and low. Classical music.

A familiar tune. He tilted his head, a bemused smile stretching his lips. One of the tunes he'd line-danced to with Roxane at Clay's wedding.

He pulled his foot off the step and walked slowly through the dark hall, noticing now that there was a dim light coming from the ballroom doorway.

He stepped in. Strings of lights around the windows bathed the tables and decorations in a romantic glow. His eyes swept the room. He'd assumed at first Roxane was playing the music on purpose, but he didn't see her.

Until she moved from the shadows.

His breath caught.

Not because she was particularly beautiful, although he thought she was.

But because of the little flirty smile that hovered around the corners of her mouth.

He swallowed through a suddenly dry throat.

Belatedly he got his own feet to move, meeting his wife in the center of the open floor. He couldn't seem to find his tongue, and all the words he wanted to say flew out of his head.

Except, "Maybe the lady would like to learn to dance?" He hoped she was recreating Clay's wedding and that he wasn't reading everything wrong.

"Maybe the lady would like to teach the man to dance."

"Ah, Boston is back." He could hear it in her tone and see it in her arched brow. "Maybe the fancy lady won't be able to teach this clumsy plowboy he has anything other than two left feet."

Her smile shot tingles clear to his toes where they bounced around, shocking and burning, until they fired their way back up his spine and out his fingers.

She stepped closer, taking his hand and putting it on her waist.

"I like your way better already," he said, humor and heat coloring his tone.

They clasped hands, and she put her other hand on his shoulder. The steps she taught him were simple, and he caught on without too much trouble. Or maybe they were just made to be together. The music flowed around them as their bodies moved together, but Roxane didn't relax into him.

Several minutes went by before she spoke. "I'm sorry."

"That's what this is? An apology?"

She nodded.

"You're setting a pretty high bar." His hand tightened on her waist. "You can apologize like this any time."

She lifted that brow.

"But you don't need to. Love covers a multitude of sins."

A wrinkle appeared between her eyes. "And that means?"

He took a fortifying breath, spiked with her classic scent. "It's just a Bible quote. It means...when you love someone, you overlook offenses."

Her eyes fluttered and then widened, searching his. He didn't quit their slow movements, but he put both arms around her. "I love you. If you need to hear it, I forgive you, too." He shook his head. "But I don't see anything that needs to be forgiven. If anything, it thrills my heart to know how deeply you loved our child. You're an amazing mother. And it's kind of crazy how we ended up together, but these last few days apart have shown me how much I've missed you, how much I've wanted you with me, how much I...love you."

He quit dancing, and his hands came up to cup her face, his thumbs brushing at the corners of her eyes. "You're leaking."

She snort-laughed. Through the smile and the tears, she said, "I don't deserve you, but I love you too, you crazy man."

He bent his head and touched her lips with his, hot and sweet and everything that he remembered.

She pulled back. "I know someplace we can go." Her whisper was husky and low, and his stomach jerked and swirled.

He put his cheek against her temple. "Are you sure?"

She nodded.

"I'm probably not going to be any better—"

She put a finger over his lips. He kissed it.

"We have the rest of our lives to practice." She took her hands from his shoulders and held his face. "I wouldn't want it any other way. It's the best way."

He looked down into her eyes and saw the truth shining in them. It was the best way, because it was God's way, but maybe, after the marriage she'd had, it really was the best way to heal her heart and help her trust.

"I'm gonna trust you on that," he said softly before he lowered his head and kissed her again.

ROXANE FLEW AROUND the house; guests had started arriving, and she wanted to make sure everything was perfect. Boone, of course, would not be upset if the evening was a total disaster, but she wanted to give him a reason to be proud of her. Not that he wasn't. She was pretty sure he thought the world of her, but still. She loved him, and she wanted him to have a wife who did her very best. At everything.

Glancing out the window as she hurried by, she saw more cars pulling in. Hopefully they had enough food. It would be awful to run out, on their first—and last—Thanksgiving meal they hosted here at Sweet Water Ranch.

The thought made her sad, so she didn't dwell on it. She'd think about it later, when the pressure of the meal was off.

"Hey, Boston, there you are." Her husband wrapped his arm around her and put a gentle kiss at one of the sensitive spots he'd discovered under the angle of her jaw.

She shivered. "We have too many people in our house for you to be kissing me there."

"I just wanted to be sure all your attention was on me."

She stopped, throwing her brain in neutral and turning to face him full-on. It wasn't any good to have the party be a success if her husband felt neglected. "It is."

"Good. Can we spare a few minutes? The lawyer for the will is here. I have him waiting in the library."

Her stomach dropped. But she shook it off. "Sure. It won't take long to tell him he can have the ranch and money."

"That's what I thought."

They shared a wordless look of complete confidence before he took her hand and walked quickly to the library.

The little man with the funny spectacles that she remembered from the night of the auction stood by the fireplace, a folder in his hand. He turned when they walked in.

Boone shut the door. "You can sit if you want to, sir, but I don't need this to take a bunch of time. I don't want the ranch and I don't want the money if it means I have to leave my wife." Boone spoke with complete assurance. His words made her heart feel warm and safe.

"I feel the same way," she said, not hesitating either. "I don't want the money or the ranch. I'm staying with my husband. You can give us a date to move out. I'll need at least two weeks."

The little man blinked, his eyes owllike behind the glasses on his nose. "Well, I must say that was unexpected. For me. Considering how things went at the auction."

Roxie wasn't sure what to think of that. If the man thought they weren't going to make it at the auction, he would have really thought they were over if he knew she lost the baby. The thought sent a pang through her. But it also scared her just a bit. She'd almost ruined every-thing.

"Well, this is going to take a little longer than you thought." He set his folder down on the desk and nodded at the chairs. "You two better sit down. You passed the test."

Epilogue

Abner held up one of the two spoons he was holding. "Blue Jello." He held up the other one. "Red Jello." He put them both in his mouth, swished them around, then opened. "Purple Jello."

None of the ladies in attendance at the Thanksgiving meal would appreciate seeing the contents of his mouth, but the kids surrounding him at the table oohed and aahed, then grabbed their plates and headed back toward the dessert table.

Abner grinned. He'd always loved kids. Had hoped to have a pile of his own. Hadn't happened.

Boone walked by, carrying two plates of dessert. Abner nodded at him as the kids straggled back with scoops of blue and red Jello on their plates. Abner couldn't help watching as Boone set a plate down in front of his wife with a gentle touch to her cheek and a whispered word in her ear.

Boone had told Abner they'd lost their baby, which hurt Abner's heart. Still, his friend was obviously in love with his wife, and it wasn't hard to see she loved him back just as fiercely.

Abner was happy for them and really didn't even think too much about the woman he'd never get over. Not anymore.

His phone buzzed in his pocket, and he almost let it go. After all, everyone he loved and cared for in the world was right here in this room. The harvest crew had finished up the last job and winterized their equipment, making it to Sweet Water just in time for this meal. The boys would be heading out to their respective homes, and Luke would be traveling back to New Zealand.

But they were all here tonight.

It was probably a telemarketer, but Abner pulled the phone out of his pocket anyway.

His heart pinged as he recognized the area code. Not the number. He hadn't called or spoken with anyone from his childhood home in Ohio for almost ten years. But he'd recognize the area code from southern Ohio for the rest of his life. Childhood memories only seemed to get stronger with age.

His whole body, led by his heart, wanted to decline the call and shove the phone back into his pocket, but his brain told him it could only be an emergency.

Did he even want to know?

He grinned at the kids who were looking at him with their mouths open, showing him their purple Jello, then he shoved his chair back from the table and straightened out of his seat, swiping his phone. He wasn't going to hide from whatever it was.

"Yeah," he said as he pushed through the door and out into the hall that led to the patio and garden. It was cold, even more since the sun went down, but he'd welcome it, probably need it.

"Abner?"

He didn't recognize the voice, but that wasn't surprising.

"Yeah."

"It's Doug."

His half brother. He'd just been a teen when Abner left.

Abner didn't say anything. Waiting.

"Gram died." Doug didn't try to break it gently. "I thought you'd want to know."

Abner's heart clenched. No wonder it hadn't wanted him to answer the phone. A call from his childhood area code could only mean hurt for his heart. "Thanks."

"Viewing's day after tomorrow, funeral the next. I'm gonna try to be in for the funeral." He paused. Abner didn't try to fill the silence with useless chatter. "It would make Mom happy if you came in." There was more silence. Some rustling came over the line, like Doug was fidgeting. "She'd really like to see you."

Abner held his phone to his ear, but his eyes were on the vast North Dakota night. Deep darkness. Crisp, clean air. Thousands of stars sparkling overhead and miles and miles of nothing man-made. If a fellow couldn't lose himself out there, going home wasn't the solution, either.

"Think you'll make it? I'll tell Mom." Doug wasn't exactly pleading, but he was a man who loved his mother.

"Doubt it." If he showed up, he wasn't going to do it with bells and whistles and a big parade. He wouldn't want to give Cora any warning. If she were still there, in his small, rural hometown. Heck, he didn't know. He hadn't talked to anyone since he'd walked. And Cora was the main reason he'd left.

No. That wasn't really true. He'd walked because he couldn't take the heartache. He wasn't sure he was any more immune now. After all, if his heart had its way, he'd never have answered this call.

"Okay. Well, I wanted to tell you." Doug stuttered a little, like he was nervous and wanted to get away.

Abner remembered a young boy, eager to please but neglected like Abner had been. There had been bad blood between them, and it took guts for Doug to call him now.

Compassion, along with something else he couldn't name, rose up in his chest, pushing his own hurt aside.

"I appreciate your call, Doug. Glad you had my number and thought of me."

"I always think of you," Doug said, not quite eagerly. "I was a jerk, and you were nice to me anyway."

Suddenly, curiosity hit Abner hard, right in the chest. What had he missed since he left? How were the ragged and scattered pieces of his mixed-up family? And Cora.

He lifted his eyes to the night sky, brilliant and beautiful. More than anything, he wanted to see Cora.

Everyone thought they'd been lovers. They hadn't.

No one realized she was his worst enemy. And he'd loved her anyway.

Still did.

THANKS FOR READING!

Abner's book, *Cowboys Don't Marry Their Enemy*, is next.

Reviews are welcome and appreciated!

Made in the USA
Monee, IL
26 July 2020